NOW LEAD ME HOME

Books by Roy Holland

Insights and Outsights: Poems by Roy Holland
>Cape Town: David Philip. ISBN: 0864861214

Just A Bit Touched: Tales of Perspective
>Writers Club Press.   ISBN: 0-595-15874-9

Flakes of Dark and Light: Tales from Southern Africa and Elsewhere
>Writers Club Press.   ISBN: 0-595-17423-X

Pivot of Violence: Tales of the New South Africa
>Writers Club Press.   ISBN: 0-595-15821-8

News From Parched Mountain: Tales from the Karoo in the new South Africa
>Writers Club Press. ISBN: 0-595-14612-0

*The Waking & Making of Paul Gauguin –
Conversations with Himself: A Play for Voices*
>Diadem Books, 2008

Alan Paton Speaking: The Lintrose Conversations
>Edited by Charles Muller. Diadem Books, 2008.

The Jonathan Three (published by Diadem Books):

The Nowhere Man   ISBN: 978-0-9559741-0-6
Journey Towards Himself   ISBN: 978-0-9559741-1-3
Now Lead Me Home   ISBN: 978-0-9559741-2-0

NOW LEAD ME HOME

THE JONATHAN THREE: VOLUME 3

Roy Holland

DIADEM BOOKS

Published by Diadem Books

For information, please contact:

Diadem Books
Ocean Surf
CLASHNESSIE
IV27 4JF
Scotland UK

www.diadembooks.com

This is a work of fiction. Characters and situations are entirely a result of the author's imagination.

ISBN: 978-0-9559741-2-0

1

After coming down from Cambridge, he had worn through a whole new typewriter ribbon copying out his Curriculum Vitae.

He had got sick of writing the same dates and the same qualifications *and* saying what school *and* what university had done for him, *and* what he wanted to do in future, *and* why he was applying for each particular job, *et cetera.*

Finally, he had got so disgusted with typing the same boring guff that he had given it up and said, he was uneducable, that he had learned nothing at school, little at university, and was now ready to pass on his ignorance and resistance to generations of students – should the Governors of the particular College be irresponsible enough to appoint him to the vacant post.

This letter of application had met with such signal success that he had been shortlisted, congratulated on his "grand sense of humour" and offered the job.

He protested that he had not been trying to be funny, but had simply told the truth. The interviewing board had thought this was funnier than ever and told him he would be a great success with the students.

So, reluctantly, he had allowed himself to accept the post. It wasn't what he desired, of course. He was still looking for an advertisement that said: ARNOLD JONATHAN GODLEY WANTED – TO BE HIMSELF. (No longer at an astronomical salary, but at any salary.)

But this one would do in the meantime.

That was how he had come to be appointed as an Assistant Lecturer in English (Probationary) at a Teachers' College for training women how to cook things and to make things to wear.

When his next of kin had been informed, Godley Senior had been pungent and direct, although he had clearly made an effort to end on a charitable note:

"It'll kill you inside six months, and serve you right, yuh daft yin! I'll offer you ten to one on the date of your funeral. Are you on?"

He should have taken the bet. He would, at least, have had some beer-money.

"How's it goin', son?" said his father one day, some weeks later.

"What?"

"Using recipe books to teach 'em the Queen's English – by means of?"

"We use proper textbooks."

"How'd you find words like chitt'lings and artichokes and scratchin's in books like that, then?" and his father cackled in high amusement.

After six months, Jonty didn't feel actually dead. He was in a transitional stage, non-human, more insectivorous – like a young bluebottle that had been sentenced to march from one end of a long and very sticky flypaper to the other, wearing a Swedish frame-rucksack, heavily packed, and having to begin in an upward direction.

Yes, that's how it felt!

At present, he was about two centimetres above his starting point. If he stuck insectfully to his task, and had normal luck, he'd just about reach the other end in time to expire, without even having the strength to collect the mandatory retirement clock with its cuckooing birds inside.

That didn't seem much of a prospect for a Godley, did it?

It would be easier to give up and die now. But that would have proved his father nearly right, and he couldn't have that either, could he?

On the whole, he felt he had reached the best solution, which was: 'Drink a lot o' beer as often and as long as you can.'

At the moment, he was following his own advice to the letter, but if things got worse, he would amend it to: 'Drink a lot of beer oftener and longer than you can.'

As the evening went by, he began to think that the second version was preferable to the first.

"You are a good beer," he said to his beer. "You're making me drunk, better, easier and faster. I'd prefer to add "and cheaper". Whass your name?"

When his beer didn't reply, he looked around the pub for a sign and saw it was a well-known South Eastern brew that claimed it had more hops in it than the others.

It was sharper than the Cambridge kind, more like the Bletchley type, maybe even one and the same. Not that taste was central to beer-drinking; it was more of a side-effect, a natural hazard.

It always had to be remembered that the essential function of beer was to make you drunk, and nothing more.

He'd learned that much from Smitty.

If it did it efficiently, the taste, whatever it was, was bound to be better than tea, coffee, mead, polishing sherry, methylated spirits, mineral water, bath water, or any other kind of liquid you could mention. Besides, he fondly maintained, doing you far less harm than such other beverages.

"Cheers!" he said to his glass, and took another appreciative swallow.

Jonty had been out on his tutorial duties, during a period of School Practice, as it was called.

He had been to assess a demonstration lesson of Miss Waugh's. She was one of the more entertaining of the student-teachers, as well a being easier on the eyes than most of them.

Nonetheless, what she had actually been demonstrating wasn't at all clear to Jonty. He suspected it wasn't clear to Miss Waugh, either; however, as her visiting tutor, it was his job to assess it.

After watching Miss Waugh, he had paid the usual courtesy call to the headmaster and had been rewarded by an hour's disquisition on the intricacies of treating sick cage-birds, a subject on which the Head was an acknowledged expert. Jonty had managed to get away on an excuse that had astonished the headmaster into silence: that he had to rush home and apply a poultice to his ailing canary.

He had escaped thankfully; but the difficulty of deciding what it was he was going to assess Miss Waugh *for* had driven him, after leaving the headmaster's study, into the nearest pub.

So, here he was, mulling over the problem.

The classroom had smelled of stale bodies and cigarette smoke. Both odours seemed to emanate from the fifteen-year-olds cynically watching Miss Waugh write the heading for the lesson on the blackboard; he had caught a whiff of her scent and he guessed she was a non-smoker.

Fifteen! Astonishing!

His first impression had been of twenty or so frowsty young adults crammed into desks several sizes too small for them.

When he had entered, the deep depression situated along the front row deepened, moved backwards a row at a time, and had become general.

But he ignored it and sat on the chair which had been provided for him at the front, carefully and deliberately placed almost inside the Art Cupboard.

The class monitors had probably conspired together and decided that was where he would see least. They were right.

So it was going to be that kind of lesson, was it?

He moved his chair to where he could survey the entire room.

His opening gambit made the depression even heavier; but when the centre of it, a huge boy with a neck like a heavyweight wrestler's and bristles growing out of his nostrils, suddenly guffawed at what Miss Waugh had written on the board, it lifted dramatically.

The heading was Miss Waugh's first 'visual aid'. She knew the college tutors were supposed to be keen on them, so she had chosen to write it up in fluorescent yellow chalk.

There it was!

She stood back and scrutinised it, admiringly. In large capitals, it announced: ANCIENT ROAM. Languidly, Miss Waugh turned round to face the class.

"What are you making all that noise for, Paul?" asked Miss Waugh, sweetly.

"It's what you writ, Miss. It's wrong!" he replied unevenly, in his cracking adolescent's voice.

So Bristlenose was named Paul, was he?

If he'd climbed through the ropes in an emerald leotard and mask, under the pseudonym of the The Hooded Crusher, nobody would have blinked.

But Paul!

Aristotle would have classified that as an improbable impossibility.

However, he seemed to be good-natured enough.

Here and there, in little scattered eruptions, the class sniggered and sputtered.

"All right, Paul," said Miss Waugh evenly, "you come and do it for us."

Paul accepted at once. The triceps under his rolled-up sleeves bulged hugely as he levered himself out of his desk. The seams on his jeans tightened alarmingly over his thighs as he got up.

When he stood at the blackboard, Miss Waugh, slender and small, hardly reached his shoulder. He took the blackboard rubber she offered to him and, with deft controlled movements, erased the word ROAM. In its place, his tongue protruding with the effort, he laboriously wrote:

ROEM.

He stood back and said, proudly: "There's an E in it, Miss."

An enormous shriek of laughter took off, climbed fast, and cruised just below the cloud-ceiling. Paul had them rolling about in the aisles and no-one was more surprised than Paul.

Miss Waugh smiled sweetly – not in the least put out.

"Something still wrong, is there?" she called above the merriment. "Who can put it right?"

The laughter subsided at once. Arms like a shower of arrows shot up and stuck quivering in the air, just above their heads.

"Miss!" they called.

"Miss!"

"Miss!"

Miss chose a small girl suffering from strabismus and large glasses. She slipped out of her desk, thin as a daisy stem; and very smugly, in straight precise letters, she wrote the word again, correctly this time.

Paul watched her with great attention and detachment. When she had finished, he said, in his cracked voice and perfect good humour:

"Oh, yeah! I jus' got the E in the wrong place, thas' all, Miss!"

The girl smiled to herself with intense pleasure.

"Thank you, Carol," said Miss Waugh. "I'm glad you're wide awake. Thank you, Paul. That was a good try."

They returned to their desks, Carol slipping in easily, like a stem through a buttonhole, Paul inching his bulk in laboriously between the lid and the backrest – a size nine foot in a size three shoe.

Miss Waugh spent the next few minutes searching.

The class watched her with bated breath. They didn't want to miss what came next. After an introduction like that she could have gone out and left them in complete silence, returning after a while to take up where she had left off. She searched through her handbag, the drawers of her desk, a mountainous pile of unmarked papers, her shoulder bag: all to no avail.

So, when she couldn't find her lesson notes, carefully prepared beforehand in college, what came next was a demonstration in how to *ad lib* on ANCIENT ROAM for half an hour without knowing anything worth knowing about it.

She started by telling them what she was going to tell them about. This seemed to be about the way Romans (loosely defined) dressed, at some place and time during the Roman Empire (also, loosely defined).

Eventually, by bending, waving, weaving, balancing, pointing, curling, uncurling, shrinking, expanding, folding, stamping, squatting, stretching, posturing and talking, she tried to describe what a toga looked like.

The class was fascinated.

They had never heard of a toga and they had never had a teacher like this before. Miss Waugh was very conscious that not only had she forgotten her lesson notes, but also her visual aids. Hence, her performance.

The boys, however, had decided that her visual aids were perfect and that all those she would ever need were on Miss Waugh herself. They were entranced.

She went through a similar set of eurythmics in describing a Roman sandal. In the middle of her demonstration, she paused, very elegantly took off her slipper to show them how the strap would be fastened over a Roman sandal, if she had really had a Roman sandal to show them, but unfortunately she hadn't, and they would have to imagine where it fitted as well as imagining what it fitted on.

See?

While she moved, she kept up a running commentary and kept pointing with her long slender fingers in stylized histrionic movements to nothing in particular.

Jonty was enjoying it every bit as much as the class; but he showed enough presence of mind to check his programme in case he had come to the wrong school, on the wrong day, to watch the wrong student giving a lesson on Modern Dance instead of one on the History of Ancient Rome.

But there it was, plain as a gladiator's sword: Miss Waugh, Tuesday, 15.00 hrs, Roman History, Class 5, Hitchback Secondary Modern. Miss Waugh's subsidiary subject was undoubtedly History, and she was undoubtedly one of his troupe!

Jonty had to admit that her photogenic properties were wonderfully effective in holding the attention of both the boys and the girls.

No; attention wasn't the right description. Mesmerism was nearer to it!

They hung on to her slightest word and her smallest movement, as if their lives depended on it – quite the opposite reaction shown by the pupils he had seen an hour earlier with another of his students.

Miss Pike, a 'mature' student, nearing forty, was as straight up and down as her name suggested she should be, and as dim as a bat, into the bargain.

On checking through a set of her lesson notes for a Biology lesson about snails, he had come across the word 'seck', which was quite unfamiliar to him. When he had queried her about it, she had told him it was used as a singular noun. Jonty had replied that he could see that, but what did it mean? Miss Pike had been astonished.

"Why!" she said. "Its plural is 'secks', of course! Surely you knew that, sir!"

"Oh, you mean, seck and sex?"

"Yessir!"

"When the snails do it once, it is seck? Twice, it is sex?"

"Exactly!"

"No! I'm sorry, Miss Pike! But sex is a singular noun. We say one sex, two sex-es."

"Really? I thought you added an ess for plurals in English, Mr Jonty!"

"Generally speaking, yes! But there are exceptions, Miss Pike!"

Her scepticism bristled strongly.

This little scene was, he felt, an emblem totally representative of why, earlier in the afternoon, he had found himself nearly in the middle of a riot in her classroom.

At a quarter past two, fifteen minutes after the commencement of Miss Pike's lesson, he had headed pronto-pronto for the classroom door, and left her to do whatever she could to stave off the coup that would soon be attempted.

After that experience, Miss Waugh's lesson was a dream.

She was concluding the lesson now by writing the two words TOGA and MOSAIC on the board. Jonty was trying to work out how MOSAIC had got itself placed up there, when Miss Waugh flashed him a triumphant smile – the first indication she had given throughout the lesson that she had been aware of his presence – as if to say:

"There! Wasn't that worth an A+?"

Or was it simply a smile of nervous relief?

Perhaps MOSAIC was a vestigial memory of something in the lesson notes she had prepared and couldn't find?

But how in the name of Madame Montessori was he going to assign a grade to a lesson like that?

From one point of view, a great deal was wrong with it; from another, a great deal was brilliantly right.

Look at Class 5!

Most of them had reserves of delinquency they hadn't even drawn on yet. Give them half a chance and they would happily reduce the desks, fittings and general school furniture to handy bundles of firewood, tied up with their PT bands and gymslip girdles, and then flog them door-to-door to buy their weekend beer and smokes.

Yet Miss Waugh had not only held them completely in thrall, but (extreme of improbabilities) probably taught them SOMETHING – although exactly what that was would be difficult to define.

However, Jonty was beginning to feel that Miss Waugh had got what it takes.

True, she had taken what it took rather far; but, there she was, alive and well! And, with Class 5's willing co-operation, had ensured that she would be able to take what it takes even further next time – which Jonty felt was a pure bloody miracle!

Wasn't she worth her full A+?

Conventionally speaking, the answer was Not.

He knew that.

First, the College expected all students to prepare and keep their notes by them while the lesson was in progress. Zero for Miss Waugh!

Second, their notes should have formulated a clear aim and activity. For example: To teach the pupils about the Roman toga and sandal of 1st Century B.C. (or whenever), so that they can make some out of ricepaper.

Or something.

What happened, Miss Waugh?

Third, the lesson should have been structured with an introduction, development and conclusion, allowing due weight and time for class activities.

Miss Waugh's demonstration had none of those elements. It simply began, continued and ended with Miss Waugh. What there was, was eternally present and unambiguously there!

What was THAT worth?

Finally, most difficult of all, Miss Waugh was going to be expected to write up an account of her lesson with an objectivity approaching Sir Alexander Fleming's discovery of penicillin.

And then –?

'—Oh, JHC, what am I doing in a game like this, anyway? What do I know about teaching? Come to that, what do I know about anything? Except beer. And maybe a bit about sex. But more about beer. Sex can come later. So what about giving her an A double bloody plus, and to hell with it?'

"Drink up and have another," he said aloud to himself.

"Thanks! I will," he replied.

Jonty got up and went to the bar. It seemed a good pub to get drunk in.

Although decidedly set in the urban sprawl of Colchester, it still thought of itself as a country inn. There the traditional open fireplace, the customary dartboard, mugs hanging up behind the bar on hooks with 'George' or 'Tom' or 'Bert' painted on them, large dead fishes shiny with varnish both in and out of glass cases, and a general air of cosiness.

Best of all, there were no bar-room machines for playing games with, and no juke-boxes.

It made only one concession to the fashion of the times that Jonty could see: the mania for printed reprimands, admonitions and exhortations. This one claimed to have been composed by the Manager and said:

The Manager wishes to inform our customers that he is not
responsible for any damage or loss incurred in the general rush to
vacate these premises at closing time.

Jonty remarked on the exaggerated humour of the notice.

"Humour!" said the Manager (who was also the Barman)
scornfully. "That's the Gospel Truth, that is. You'd be surprised at
th'accidents we 'ave 'ere. Alf Jones fell off one o' them 'igh stools
th'other day, he was in such a rush to get 'ome, he sprained 'is drinkin'
lip! Why, I've even known blokes ferget to drink up, and leave a
finger or two in the bottom. It ain't natural. I can't take responsibility
fer that kind o' thing, can I?"

The Manager said this without a tremor of a smile on his dough-
coloured face. He was obviously a past master of such irony.

Jonty agreed that fingers in jars weren't healthy, just to let him
know he had understood his pun, and then remarked on the lack of
customers in the bar.

"Five thirty's too early for the reg'lars. Start coming about seven,
they do. Only the odd one with a forgivin' missus pops in on his way
'ome from work. 'Ere you are, mate!"

The barman put his foaming tankard in front of him.

"Got to slip down an' look at me pipes, now. Leave the money on
the bar."

And he was gone.

Jonty took his pint carefully back to the hearth, placed it in one of
the small ledges let into the brickwork of the fireplace and sat down on
the wheelback chair to toast his toes in the heat.

He was just about to take a long sensual pull at his beer when, who
should come into the bar but Miss Waugh?

What a dirty trick to play on your very own tutor!

He put the beer back, untouched, on its ledge and regarded her at
length.

Not only was she utterly worth regarding, but she had caught him in
the middle of trying to convince himself to let the college authorities
get screwed (as long as he didn't have to do it in person) and trying to

talk himself into awarding her an A double plus just as he was about to take a sensual gulp of beer.

How on earth could she be insouciant enough to prevent all that; while – at the same time – looking like a distillation of pure sex in scarlet pants, tight white sweater, maxi coat, blonde hair, and – simultaneously – not only attempting to, but actually succeeding in, distilling it in its utmost purity?

It wasn't fair, was it?

"Oh, Mr Godley!" she said. "I saw your vehicle in the car park. And I did so want to talk to you. I hope you don't mind?"

'Mind? How can I mind? My mind is deserting me!'

"You've changed your clothes!" he replied, irrelevantly.

"I always do that after school! It helps my morale. May I sit down?" she said, placing her hand-and-shoulder bags beside the leg of an empty wheelback.

"Of course!" he said at once, realizing that allowing her to do that did absolutely nothing for his morale, except to weaken it.

He motioned mutely to the chair.

Miss Waugh sat down.

Her scarlet pants clung to her legs like a second skin.

'Oh, my God!' he moaned inwardly. 'Don't do it like that! Pull that protracted coat over yourself, can't you? It isn't as if I'm fifty-six with thinning hair and a heavy mortgage, is it? You must be aware that I'm more than old enough and just big enough!'

"I was so upset after that awful lesson, Mr Godley, that I went straight to the Public Library and cried for half an hour in the Biology section. I felt I couldn't go back to College, just yet. So I began walking. When I spotted the College-Mini in the car park, I thought I might try to—."

She interrupted herself, impulsively.

"You do see, don't you, Mr Godley?"

'See? If you sit like that, who can help seeing? How come that there is so little of Miss Waugh but so much of IT? You're no bigger than a new ha'penny.'

"That's perfectly all right, Miss Waugh! Don't apologise. You did very well, really."

Silently, he added: 'And you're doing very well now, if you only knew it.'

"Really? Oh, Mr Godlety! Do you think so? I was so worried!"

"Don't worry! Giving a bad lesson isn't the end of the world, is it?"

"It could be the end of mine, Mr Godley!"

"How?"

"This is my final T.P. and—"

"—T.P?"

"Teaching Practice! And I've done so badly in all the others, I just HAVE to do well in this one."

He felt disappointed but could not place the reason. She fluttered her long fingers and clasped them in her lap. She lowered her head and the long blonde hair fell forward, covering her breasts.

Jonty sighed. He couldn't help it.

There was something so touchingly innocent and sexually exciting about it, that he did not trust himself to reply to her. He simply sat and looked at her.

"Miss Clatworthy says this is my last chance. And my mother will never forgive me if I get thrown out, Mr Godley. She's scraped and saved for so long to send me—."

Jonty interrupted the sequence of tortures he had begun to devise for Miss Clatworthy to wonder if he should be encouraging one of his own students to drink with him.

Firm in the knowledge that he most emphatically should not, he said: "May I offer you a drink, Miss Waugh? A treble whisky, perhaps? Or maybe a pint of Daquiri?"

Miss Waugh giggled.

"I'd love a beer," she replied.

"Then a beer you shall have," and he just managed to stop himself adding, "my lovely!"

The Manager, fresh back from tickling up his pipes, looked at him quizzically.

Miss Waugh was too diminutive to provide accommodation for a whole pint, so Jonty ordered a half.

The Manager, now Barman, put it on the counter.

"A bit of all right, that is," said the Barman.

"I think I prefer less hops in it," replied Jonty, measuring the width of its Roman collar with his eye.

"What?" said the barman in perplexity, his eyes over Jonty's shoulder.

Jonty looked up and noted with amusement that the Manager's large doughy face had taken on a more leavened expression since he had espied Miss Waugh.

"Oh, yes! I see! It is, isn't it?" said Jonty.

"It is that!" replied the manager-cum-barman, fervently.

Jonty heard raindrops begin pattering against the windows of the pub.

He looked up. The skies were slate-coloured and the light was draining out of them like greasy water.

As he carried her half pint to the hearth, he noticed with joy and desire how the firelight flickered along her thighs, arms, and the red-gold strands of her hair hanging over her breasts.

'Cer-ripes! Who cares whether her grade is A-double-plus or Z-double-minus when she can do with so little effort what she can't help doing all the time?'

Jonty realized he had reached another of those moments in his experience which made him ask what was and what wasn't important.

He was on another of his value-ranking binges that were so difficult to resolve.

Seeing Miss Waugh sitting in front of the fire like that made him realize even more forcibly what he had realized all too frequently over the last six months: how uncut-out he was for what he was being paid to do. He wasn't even good at pretending to be an Assistant Whatsit in Something-or-Other, never mind actually being it.

Was it HIS fault if what all those Old Biddies thought mattered, didn't?

And if what they thought didn't matter, did?

'What matters is what matters, and when it matters as much as it seems to matter at this very moment, well, Miss Clatworthy, damn her eyes, can stuff her rules, values and regulations into one of her self-timing ovens and baste them with her favourite gravy until they are well and truly done!'

"There you are, then," said Jonty, handing Miss Waugh her half. "That'll make you feel better."

"Thank you so much, Mr Jonty. It really is good of you to – to—"

Not knowing how to conclude, she took refuge in smiling dazzlingly at him.

Predictably, he was dazzled.

Her teeth were very white and slightly crooked. The sheer unexpectedness of her chuckle made his gonads feel as if they were taking off from Cape Kennedy on their way to orbiting Alpha Centauri.

"Tell me," he said desperately. "Had you really prepared that lesson? Because if you hadn't, you could hardly expect a class of fifteen-year-olds to—"

"—Oh, I had, I did, Mr Godley, I did! I always do. It's just that… I'm so feather-brained. I keep leaving things all over the place, and losing things. By the way, I found my lesson-folder after you'd gone. It was on my desk all the time! Would you believe it?"

And she chuckled again.

The second time, Jonty felt ready to believe anything she cared to tell him.

But he knew he had to try to preserve a proper professional stance and not keep thinking she was the liberally buttered piece of crumpet she was. That line of thought could be heavily destructive of student-teacher relationships. He must endeavour to keep things on the vocationally depressing plane of methodology, or on the oppressively suicidal level of the philosophy of didactics.

Or on – anyway, the worse the better.

"I'm glad to hear it! Anybody can give a poor lesson, now and then. Even the best—" He couldn't quite bring himself to say 'of us', so he went on: "—the best of teachers have their off-days."

"I know! But to make such a *faux pas* in front of a tutor who has specially come to—"

"—No, don't worry, Miss Waugh! I'll tell you – but strictly off the record, you understand? Must be our secret!"

She nodded her head swiftly.

"Well, I thought you were bloody marvellous! All that mime! Worked like a charm. You had them eating out of the palm of your hand."

"Do you think so?" she asked breathlessly.

"I know so! Young Paul couldn't take his eyes off you. And no wonder! After your initial mistake, of course!"

"Initial mistake? What was that?"

Jonty stopped himself halfway through a large swallow, then let it go before replying.

"Fairly obvious, wasn't it? Your mis-spelling of Rome."

"Oh, but that was the one thing in the entire lesson that went according to plan, Mr Godley!"

2

Jonty put his glass tankard into one of the niches of the fireplace and looked steadily at Miss Waugh.

"How'd you mean?" he asked. "Planned?"

"Well I knew I would never hold a class like that by normal methods. If I could somehow enlist their sympathy, I thought I might get somewhere. It was a deliberate mistake."

"You did that unmistakably!"

"What?" she asked, anxiously.

"Get somewhere! Any student who can work out a ploy like that and have the nerve to carry it through won't ever have to worry about being no good. You're a natural! In your place, I wouldn't even have thought of it!"

"Oh, Mr Godley, you're just flattering me to make me feel better, aren't you?"

'Too bloody true, I'm flattering you; but it's to make ME feel better,' he thought silently.

"Not at all, Miss Waugh! You've got what it takes!" he said.

'And I wish you'd give it to me,' thought Jonty.

He went on.

"As a teacher, I mean. You're going to be all right. The tricks of the trade, the manner, the knowledge— oh, you'll pick all that up in no time at all. But, tell me! What brought you wearing house-slippers in the classroom?"

She chuckled a third time, and took a small sip of beer, her first. The taste surprised her and she pursed her lips.

"Is it all right?" asked Jonty, anxiously.

It suddenly seemed very important to him that she should like the beer.

"Oh, yes, fine! You see, we'd just had a P.E. lesson and—"

"—What?"

"Physical Education!"

"Of course! Silly me!"

"And I just hadn't bothered to take them off again."

"I see. What would Miss Nightingale have to say about that? Do you always wear house-slippers for P.E?"

She giggled again.

"No. I couldn't find my pumps. You see, I always bring slippers."

Jonty was perplexed and showed it.

"To put on in the staffroom – during free periods! They give my feet a rest," she explained patiently.

"Oh!"

Neither of them felt the remarks needed adding to, so they sat looking into the fire for a moment.

Jonty found himself sipping his beer in small pecking movements – a sign he was unsettled – and, as he did so, glancing from the corner of his eye, and pondering the way the firelight flushed the thrusting roundness of Miss Waugh's breasts through the rose-whiteness of her sweater.

Were they to be classed as doopers, or super-doopers? They certainly belonged to one or the other group, and they had not been borrowed or padded out as an after-thought.

Or should that be as fore-thoughts?

Maybe they would turn blue litmus paper red? Or vice versa?

He realized that the beer and the heat were loosening him up, but he was embarrassed to find Miss Waugh watching him watch her. To hide his chagrin, he took a noisy gulp of the hop-boosted brew.

In response, she stood up suddenly, removed her maxi-coat and threw it over the back of a vacant chair. Involuntarily, his eyes again began outlining her shape.

"I shan't get the benefit of it later on, if I wear it now," she said. "This fire's lovely!"

"I hope you don't go into classrooms in those things, Miss Waugh!" he said, to distract himself

"Which things?" she asked sweetly.

"Those pants."

"Oh, no! We aren't allowed to. Miss Clatworthy insists on dresses or skirts. I always get changed after school into something a bit more swinging than the – the—"

"—I know! A good job, too!" he added miserably.

"What?"

"Nothing! Just thinking aloud, How's your beer?"

"It's nearly finished. But—"

"—Have another."

"Don't you think I oughtn't? Shouldn't I get back, Mr Godley? To College?"

"Do you want to? Because I can give you a lift."

"I don't WANT to! I just thought I ought to. You know – preparing tomorrow's lessons; writing up today's reports; resting. That sort of thing!" she added vaguely.

"Well, it's your decision!"

"There are no tutors coming in tomorrow, I hope!" She looked at him, slyly. "Are there?"

"No idea! I'm certainly not!"

"Oh, I'll stay, then! I can write my reports tomorrow – in my free periods. Yes, I will, please! The same again."

He went to the bar for another half and a new pint for himself. He took them both back to the hearth.

They still had the bar-room to themselves. She took her glass from him and raised it slightly in salute before taking a small sip of the froth. Then, apparently comfortable in his presence, she gazed wistfully into the fire, quite still and silent, the glass poised in her lap.

Jonty sat down, said nothing, and took a large pull of the fresh beer.

It was his third fill: he was beginning to feel solid and real once more.

Pretending to be what he wasn't placed a heavy strain on his nervous system; watching Miss Waugh in front of the flames, her soul's self contained within herself, the firelight etching in her body's outlines, and pretending not to want to do what he most incontestably did want to do, also put him under a strain, albeit of a more satisfying kind.

It was a bloody good thing that booze helped both kinds!

One of the reason beer ranked high in the spectrum of Jonty's pleasure was that he had not yet found an end to the uses he could put it to.

Just think of its properties!

It was wet; it made you happy; sad; sleepy; unconscious; funny; bitter; ecstatic; merry; tiddly; drunk; paralytic; uncompromising – there was no end to what it could do! And not least was the fact that it was a liquid and you could actually drink it in places solely devoted to selling it.

There was no doubt that Brits had got some things right and 'The Pub' was one of them!

"Do you mind if I ask you a personal question, Mr Godley?" Her voice broke unexpectedly into his encomium on the virtues of John Barleycorn.

'Not I if it's the one I've been considering,' he thought.

"Depends on what it is, Miss Waugh," he said aloud.

"Well, we were wondering – we always do – you know, the girls in my hostel – if you were married, Mr Godley?"

Jonty felt sure that Miss Clatworthy must have placed matters like these, as topics of conversation between student and tutor, utterly out of bounds. Most of her rules encouraged blindness to anything you couldn't happily raise in vestry meetings at tea-time.

Should he now, as one of THEM, take out his tutor's whistle, blow it, and shout 'Foul'? Or should he—? While he was wondering how to reply, Miss Waugh went on:

"Spouses pop in and out all the time. It's quite interesting!... I asked because we haven't seen your wife about the College, Mr Godley."

'Well, it's not surprising, is it?' thought Jonty. 'I haven't seen her about there myself.'

"Yes," he answered. "As a matter of fact, I am. But we're separated."

"Oh! I'm sorry!"

"Don't be sorry! It wasn't your fault!"

Miss Waugh looked at him queerly for a moment, and then stared into the fire again. The silence was brief for, at that moment, a group of thirsty dart players came into the bar and began to organise themselves pints of beer and group themselves into two teams.

Soon, their chatter and the clunk of darts relentlessly going into the board, punctuated his thoughts.

'Now, why did I say that?

'It's the first I've heard about Sofia and me being separated!

'Of course, in a way it's true. She buggered off from Cambridge months ago.

'But it isn't true in the way this girl's going to think it's true, is it?

'No; it is not.

'So why this "matter of fact" bullshit? As a matter of bullshit! As a bullshit of bullshit! What about – as horseshit of horseshit? Aitch ess of bee ess? That at least would be concrete, graphic and honest.

'Am I gradually turning into one of them?'

The suspicion greatly upset Jonty's composure and, under some duress, he took another large pull at his tankard.

He felt the draught slew his brain round to a more normal position in his skull and his interior conversation became consecutive again, but it unexpectedly formed itself into a set of Clatworthy-type ordinances:

'I must try to stop,' it went, 'treating Miss Waugh as a fully human adult woman and try treating her as the fully unformed student she is, as defined by the fully professional Miss C.'

'I must try to endure in silence and stillness the grumbling-and-grunting activities she stimulates me to perform, without actually grumbling and grunting out loud, or performing them.'

'I must try to stop giving the impression I'm one of the indispensable kirbigrips in the balding crown of education.'

'I must try to stop feeling what I feel because I feel it, and stop saying what I think because I think it.'

'Amen.'

Jonty beheld himself helplessly caught in the grip of his speculations, but strongly disagreed with the formulations they had fallen into. Since Miss Waugh's entry into the arena, they had developed a momentum of their own.

First, that hot steaming nonsense about his separation from Sofia; now these freshly-dropped dollops of wisdom from his censor!

None of THEM were victimised by their own thoughts, were they? They wouldn't allow it! Oh, dear no! Little wonder that 'them that flourish' flourished, and went on blithely doing it!

'It's only people like me who keep shovelling that destructive brand of manure round their own roots,' he thought miserably.

It was at this point that something irresistibly prompted him to begin telling her all about his relationship with Sofia and their marriage, and about his father and the fortune he had won on the football pools, and how his father wanted to start a betting shop with Jonty as one of the bookies, and how there should be a law against the way she looked, and another law against the way he felt, and the firelight, and the dart players and the noise and the smoke and the way it was all beginning to move and. to change into something he did not want to happen and, at the same time, something he wanted very much to happen...

♣

Miss Waugh called his name.

Jonty, who was halfway across the dark square of the Pub's car park in the pelting Essex night, stopped, turned, and felt the rain hurling its grapeshot into his face.

Her voice came again.

"Arnold! I'm blind!"

"Hurry!" he said. "I'm going to unlock the car."

His emotions crackled like dry gorse. They were on fire, and smoke was filtering down his nose and tickling his ears. Amber-coloured luxury swashed and gurgled in unimaginable places a thousand miles away inside him.

He stood in the rain, as dry as a bone. The small metal key in his fingers, which he tried to put into the lock, was as large as a tennis racket. He could hear someone laughing foolishly in the wet dark and felt the spasms shaking his throat.

"Arnold!" she called again.

"Don't be silly!" he yelled. "A couple of pints don't make you blindo. Quick! I've opened the door with a tennis racket."

"I can't! You'll have to fetch me. Not blindo. Blind! Night blind!"

"Don't move!" he shouted. "I'm a dolphin, speeding through the – through the—."

The rest of the idea escaped him.

He found himself fully occupied with the attempt to get up off his knees and to keep his hands out of puddles that smelled of gearbox oil. He wiped them on his handkerchief. The gorse-fire in his head was roaring in his ears. He found that he was holding her hand. She was following him.

"It's something to do with the rods and cones," she was saying.

The wet dark night was clearing his head.

Smoke had stopped issuing from his nostrils and he was breathing air again. The crackling of the gorse had abated. Instead, now, someone was singing. First, a soprano solo; then plainsong, in the nave of his skull, cathedralled, swelling, bassbaritoned, overwhelming; but it began to come out wrong: a weird bagpipe voice, lamenting a blind girl called Valerie who had fallen in love with a beggar disguised as a Prince.

"Who's making all that noise?" he asked.

"It's you, you fool!"

She giggled, realizing what she had said, and tried to retrieve it, by adding: "Mr Godley, sir, I'm having such a lovely time. I never knew tutors were like this."

"Like what?"

"Human!"

"I'm not human!" said Jonty. "C'mon! Get in. No, silly! The other side. Don't know what I am. Unless it's a hundred and fifty proof of Holy Joy dancing through the dark mind of Satan. A tiny piece of God in the whirling spaces of the atom. I'm—"

"—Blasphemous, that's what you are!"

"I'm ecstasy. I'm sin. I'm extinction. I'm pure whisky, dead drunk in the stills. I'm the distilled essence of the waters of life. I'm—"

He flopped backwards into the driving seat of the Mini Minor.

"Whoosh!" he went on. "What a marvellous feeling to be drunk with somebody as beautiful as you!"

The rain grapeshotted on the car windows in the dark.

How peculiar! It made a noise like somebody crying.

"Listen to the rain. It sounds like crying."

The girl quivered beside him. He turned: too dark to see!

"God in heaven! What's the matter?"

"Nothing!"

She was crying.

"I'm all right, Mr Godley. Arnold. Really!"

She was crying.

He put his arm round her in the night.

"Now, come on, Val, old girl! Whatever it is – it's not that bad, is it?"

"It's just – just that – it's the nicest thing anybody has ever said to me anywhere in my whole life. I can't h-help it! I'm sorry!"

She pressed against him.

Everything suddenly stilled: the sound of her crying, the grapeshot on the panes, the whispering gorse, as quiet as the blank eye of the tornado inside him.

"Don't be sorry, girl! Sorry is something not to be. Not now. Not here."

He wasn't drunk any more. He wasn't happy. He wasn't querulous. He wasn't nothing. He wasn't anything. He was stillness. He was peace.

It was all so bloody ridiculous!

Just because of a crying girl, blind and beautiful in the dark, pressed against him, not crying any more, he felt as if he'd found the centre of what it was all about.

Perhaps he WAS still drunk? But he couldn't be THAT drunk, could he?

She lifted herself away from him to put her face up to his cheek and kiss him, timidly.

…Please God, no! NO!

"I don't care," she said. "I don't care what I'm doing. I want you to kiss me. Please, Mr Godley! Arnold!"

Oh Gawd! No. NO-OO-OO!...

Her lips were exactly as he had known they would be; and the way she came out and went in under his hands was exactly the shape he had known she would reveal; and the warmth between her thighs that moved so surely open for his fingers to probe and press and make him feel as though he was palpating the Lotus itself while her body slowly moved backwards under his weight and all the godawful lovely predictable bloody rest of it was the way he had guessed it would have to be and OUGHT to be and he didn't want it ever to stop.

After a while, he said softly: "You're drunk, Miss Waugh!"

"I know," whispered Miss Waugh. "Ditto, Mr Godley!"

"Not any more," he said.

"Please," she said. "Again! Please!"

"Don't ask! Don't say it. It weakens me."

"I will, I will!" she said fiercely. "Please, please, please..."

He found himself turning towards her and letting his weight gently down on to her. He was aware, for a moment, that the rain had again begun crying on the windscreen and falling with its little tick-tacking noises onto the roof of the car.

Then, there was only her body quivering and shuddering under him and he was putting his lips to her lips and to her cheeks and her neck and her ears and he was talking as he'd never talked before and as he never guessed he would want to talk to anybody ever in the big wide world.

But soon, he was silent and she became an unimaginable perfume that sang to him in a beautiful voice, shaped to the contours of happiness, soundlessly.

3

The next morning, before stepping into the corridor, Jonty looked cautiously out of his study door. Miss Clatworthy, who had her office on the same floor as Jonty's, was the last personage in what promised to be a grisly world that he wished to encounter today. Her door was at the head of the stairs, so that it was impossible to avoid going past it to get out of, or into, his study.

Unless, that is, he went along the corridor in the opposite direction and down the rear staircase, which was part of the Janitor's flat and forbidden as a thoroughfare.

He wondered whether, today, he shouldn't risk it, because, although it was a bright January morning, it was still raining inside his head: a steady downpour of liver spots that jigged and jigged in front of his eyes; and, although he was actually vertical, he felt himself to be all hunched up in front of the ghostly windows of an empty house, waiting for an endless winter storm to go away.

Even the small varnished plate on her door frightened him this morning: it just went on relentlessly announcing MISS M. CLATWORTHY PRINCIPAL in, what seemed to Jonty, terribly black, unmistakably assertive capital letters.

It was a minute or two after nine.

Every morning, dead on the stroke of the hour, Miss Clatworthy brought her narrow, corseted ideas to her large airy office and installed them behind a desk as high as a pulpit. To Jonty, she was the Original Super-Droopered Puritan Conscience. He was hoping she had been as punctual today as she usually was, so that he could get out unseen.

She embodied for him all the childish nightmares, marathon canings for scrumping, unendurable shakings for peeing over the walls of the girls' lavatories, all the YOU WONT'S, YOU CANT'S and THOU SHALT NOTS he had ever heard of, and all the dark ugly faces of AUTHORITY he had ever seen.

Whenever Miss Clatworthy's eyes fell on Jonty, her heavy lips turned themselves into a long white hyphen, and he half-expected her to invite him into her office to receive a good dressing down for not only allowing himself to be called Jonty, but also for actually being Jonty, as well as for admitting it in public.

But, so far, she never had. In fact, when she had had occasion to speak to him, she had always been very pleasant and polite. Jonty simply supposed she could no longer resist – it was such an ingrained habit – tightly buttoning up her double-breasted chin, even when she felt amiable towards him.

Nevertheless, friendly or not, she remained for Jonty an entity to be avoided at all costs.

That was why he was walking softly towards the stairhead on tiptoe, hoping fervently she was, at that very moment, deep in the current edition of *The Watchtower*.

He had reached the top stair and had put his hand to the banister when he heard, with a toppling stomach, the door opening behind him. He forced himself to keep looking ahead and, with immense control, had managed to overcome his instant paralysis, kept moving, and had gone down four steps before she called him.

"Oh, Mr Godley!"

'Great balls of owl-shit! May the—'

A heavy clumping platoon of foot-oaths marched towards articulation, but he checked them, allowing them to filter bluely but soundlessly into the chaste college air.

Jonty turned.

"Yes, Miss Clatworthy?"

An imposing fifty-eight year old virgin in an expensively cut suit of Air Force blue stood in the doorway of her office with an expression like an English preacher who has strayed into a Bethesda brothel by mistake.

"I'd like a word with you, if I may, Mr Godley, about—"

She paused significantly.

'—Changing my name? Fibre-moulded teacups for schools? Rubber buttons on cami-knickers?—'

"—About one of our students," she added.

Panic swept over him.

They've tortured her! They've force-fed her on gallons of senna and she's told them the truth in the toilet!

'Ignominy! Disgrace! The Shame of the Regiment! It's all caught up with me at last!'

"Oh, yes? Certainly," he said aloud, in agonies of alarm.

"It's about Miss Pike. She worries me, Mr Jonty."

'Miss Pike!... Christ, not half as much as she worries me! But – Miss Pike – my guardian angel! Thank God for Miss Pike! Go down on your knees, boy, and whisper, over and over, "Miss Pike, Miss Pike, with a voice like a shrike", until it becomes a hymn of love and adoration. Say nice things when you see her. Treat her as if she's clean-shaven. Smile at her five o'clock shadow. Be big-hearted! She's saved your bacon, you ungrateful—!'

"—Come in and sit down, Mr Jonty."

'I don't like the way she said that. You can tell she used to sing in a choir, can't you?'

She turned her metre-wide rump to him (square at the corners) and, with her shoulders back, marched in short firm strides, on block-heeled shoes, with polished toes, back to her pulpit.

'Ah well,' thought Jonty, 'if I'm going to get a bollocking, I'd rather get it sitting down than standing up. It'll prevent them falling round my ankles.'

As he followed her into the office, a whiff of antiseptic caught him unawares.

Was it carpet-shampoo, or personal hygiene?

Miss Clatworthy seated herself, her back to the light, on her swivel chair and prepared herself to be The Principal.

Jonty couldn't see all the transformations clearly because of the brightness coming through the large bow windows behind her and the constant drizzle of liver spots that speckled his vision; but, for one thing, he got the impression that she was settling her head further back on its neck and manufacturing another chin.

'Some people will try anything to hide a spotty skin. What she needs is—'

"—How is she getting on, Mr Jonty, at her school?"

She sounded angry.

Jonty hoped she wasn't, because her large imposing face turned purple round the dewlaps, and shook, and she gobbled like a turkey when she lost her temper.

Was it anger suffusing her pimples now, in the shadows, or was his vision playing tricks again?

"Well—," he began, hesitantly.

"—I want to be frank with you, Mr Godley. I'm worried. I may even sound a little brutal. But then I must be. I'm a guardian of Government money. I have been told, by Matron, that Miss Pike is eating – well, not to beat about the bush – like a horse. I find this extraordinary. She's as thin as a rake, Mr Godley!"

'As a pike, Miss Clatworthy, made of wood and metal,' amended Jonty, in his mind.

"She also appears to have – er – somewhat unsavoury personal habits – in the dormitories. And, yesterday, on the telephone, I was informed by the Headmaster of her school—"

'—That boring bloody expert on avian epidemics!'

"—that she has actually claimed in the staffroom, Mr Godley, where everyone could hear, and in a very loud voice, to have strong connexions with Mau-Mau!"

"What?"

"I don't wonder you're surprised, Mr Godley. Yes, I know she's old enough, even though she isn't yet a mature woman. But Mau-Mau! It's a little odd, isn't it?"

'Well, good on you, hen!' he thought.

"It certainly is, Miss Clatworthy."

"She hasn't, I understand, claimed to know Jomo Kenyatta PERSONALLY, but I believe her parents were in Africa, at some time or other. Have you noticed anything strange about her, Mr Godley?... Now, you can be quite frank with me."

"Well—"

"—Yes?"

"Not exactly strange, Miss Clatworthy. But, I'd say – er – stupid."

"Ah! For instance, Mr Jonty?"

"I remarked the other day that she had missed out the author's name, in her lesson notes, of a book she was reading aloud to the children and—"

"—Yes?"

"When I asked her who it was, she looked at the book's title-page, and told me it was written by—"

"—Go on!"

"She said: 'By J.M. Dent & Sons Ltd."

"Ha, ha! Did she? She wasn't trying to be funny, I hope?"

"No, not Miss Pike! On this occasion, she was very grateful to learn of her mistake."

"Well, that's something in her favour. Anything else, Mr Godley?"

Should he mention the lesson on Ghana when she had, in the face of strong evidence that it was practised only in New Guinea and by New York psychiatrists, given the children the most detailed instructions he had come across so far on how to shrink heads?

And how, afterwards, she had threatened she would shrink any child's head who put a foot wrong to the size of a pea and display it over the blackboard?

"No! I don't think so, Miss Clatworthy," he said.

"Dress? There's no substitute for a good appearance, Mr Jonty."

'There's no substitute for Miss Pike, either,' thought Jonty.

"I quite agree, Miss Clatworthy. But she dresses neatly, on the whole."

"Punctuality?"

Jonty shook his head.

"I'm not aware of anything untoward."

"Well, I'm rather relieved, really. Thank you, Mr Godley. We'll see how she gets along with the rest of her Teaching Practice, then."

Jonty had learned that when Miss Clatworthy thanked him, she was giving him a signal to dismiss. He stood up at once.

"If that is all, Miss Clatworthy, I'll be—"

"—Are you feeling more settled here, now? It must be difficult for you – a women's Housecraft College?"

Prolonging the interview with inquiries about his state of mind? Odd!

Normally, she seemed to assume he hadn't got one. Was she feeling better disposed towards him? Why?

"Not at all! I'm hoping to learn how to cook and sew and knit, in due course."

"Oh, really? Ha, ha! Well, good morning, Mr Godley."

"Good morning, Miss Clatworthy."

He scuttled out of her office and down the stairs three at a time, heading for the Library.

He was very glad that she hadn't decided to run through all the things she was for and against in her staff and her students, demanding that he tick them off one by one against Miss Pike's record in particular.

Anyway, he knew them by heart.

How could he not?

He had heard them repeated so many times already in Staff Meetings (and Miss Clatworthy often looked straight at Jonty when she recited them – especially the one about acceptable lengths of hair) that it would be difficult to forget them.

He reached the bottom of the stairs and walked out of the building into the sunshine.

Then, on the instant, he changed his mind about the Library: he'd go the pool in the grounds, to calm his nerves.

He could look out the books he needed for his lecture on the Seventeenth Century Metaphysicals, later.

Shades of Redshins!...

He began to recall him with comparative affection.

Redshins!

There was no mistaking what HE had been in favour of, although he had never explicitly defined it: simply knowing about, thinking about, and doing what he could about SEX, in all its literary and situational contexts.

Redshins! the very word was like a bell to toll me back....

And there was no mistaking what Miss Clatworthy was in favour of: NOT knowing about, NOT thinking of, or DOING anything about sex at all, regardless of its context.

Her practical housecraft mind simply sewed up, in hessian sacking, blanket stitch, and heavy nylon thread, all references to sexual congress and its cohorts and dropped them, with her appropriate weights of disapproval, into the sea of forbidden topics that surrounded the inaccessible island she had built her College on. Singlehanded, she accounted for the fact that students generally found great difficulty in finding any book that was normally informative on plant or animal reproduction in the Hygiene, Biology and General Science sections of the College Library; or indeed, in the entire College.

As George Upall, the Art & Craft Lecturer put it: "She thinks Geography is about maps; History about chaps; and Hygiene about claps."

Educational films, for use in College or schools, on the breeding habits of any living or extinct species of anything, were unheard of.

Also, she accounted for the fact that her students had no accommodation (even furnished with two straight-backed chairs and an ashtray) called VISITORS' ROOMS, where they could take their dates to.

Further, it accounted for the fact that in Spring and Summer you could find them and their boyfriends, late at night, standing up, sitting down, or even lying full-length, in the rhododendron beds at the front of the College; and, in Winter, supine on the dried leaves, moving as fast as they could to keep warm.

It was generally understood that 'the pill' was something you took only for constipation.

Despite all this (or, more probably, because of all this) pregnancies were fairly common, but they were never mentioned in open country.

Oh, dear no!

There was no doubt that Miss Clatworthy was doing more than her bit to curb the 'copulation explosion'. Consciously or unconsciously, she was trying to restrain the world's breeding activities in the little bit of South East Essex she was responsible for.

It was, thus, a matter of some surprise to Jonty that she hadn't yet been snapped up by WHO or UNESCO. She would have been a godsend to the world that had still to be taught that the meaning of survival was continence, wouldn't she?

With such misgivings in his mind, was it to be wondered that Jonty this morning was feeling vulnerable?

What would Miss C. do with Mr G. if she knew what Mr G. had done last night with Miss W?

The mere consideration was enough for Jonty to imagine that, from sheer anxiety, his hair was going to fall out; and with alopesia he'd look even more ridiculous to Miss C. than he did already, besides becoming an immediate object for her suspicions.

Would he be forced to disguise it – perhaps with a wig like Big Rev's, the lecturer in Religious Knowledge?

Or, on second thoughts, as unlike Big Rev's as possible!

'Oh, God! What a world to land myself in!

'Why did I ever take the job?

'Most of it was already in evidence at the interview.

'That funny wizened little Divisional Education Officer who asked me if I knew what I'd do if one of the students set her cap at me.

'Oh, yes, I knew what I'd do, all right!

'The little man had been satisfied with the mere assurance…

'Well, I was right, wasn't I? I had done it. Last night. In the rain. In a Mini Minor. And that's no mean feat! In *locus parentis*. Drunk!'

And here he was, in broad daylight the following day, working for, and actually speaking to MISS M. CLATWORTHY, PRINCIPAL; who was against – apart from sex – dances, trimmings at Christmas, alcohol, permissive behaviour, abortion, radical thinking, coffee-drinking, pot, amphetamines, long hair, sleeping pills, sleeping partners, blue films, LSD, tobacco, books, and everything to do with the British Labour Party.

While, with no sense of strain, and simultaneously, she was FOR autocracy, *Blackwood's Magazine*, going to church (not ANY church), getting in on time, speaking up in a big voice in the classroom, not speaking at all in Staff Meetings, dressing modestly, dressing neatly, washing behind the ears before school, short nails, long skirts, keeping busy (especially when you had nothing to do), being nice (even to people no self-respecting person ought to be nice to), bathing everything daily, being very very nice to 'nice people' (whether you liked them or not), tying up your hair neatly, having it cut regularly, anything that provided a challenge, going to bed early, prayers, getting up early, and the daily ironing of smalls (even for men).

It was a good thing he had got a degree from Cambridge or he wouldn't have understood these things, would he?

What was making everything worse was the letter he had found in his pigeonhole that morning, when he had arrived in College to start preparing his lectures on the Metaphysicals.

Having had little time to consider all the implications of what had happened between him and Valerie, or even time to feel joy or remorse, he was not only faced with the greatest onslaught of liver spots he had ever experienced, but now he had received a summons to go to Birmingham next weekend and to discuss with Sofia their arrangements for getting a divorce.

They say that troubles don't come singly. These could be the harbingers of a charabanc party.

He reached the poolside.

The place was deserted.

No-one was swimming: at this time of the year, the water was still too cold. It glinted its oblong blue eye at him. The grass banks plumped themselves up like large timid bolsters edging away from the biscuit-coloured paving slabs that surrounded the pool.

He selected one of the circular metal tables freshly painted in white placed at the top of a green bank, with its nest of wrought iron chairs, also in new coats, and removed the top one, placed it at the table and sat in it.

The breeze was fresh. The breath of the sea was on it, sweeping up the estuary of the River Colne, inland.

He inhaled deeply.

It helped. He was thankful that he had the place to himself. Another help.

He took out Sofia's letter to read it again. He had to hold both edges firmly to prevent it blowing out of his hands.

How had she found out his address? She asked to see him in Birmingham, at Crehan's.

Why couldn't she come to Colchester?

No. Perhaps it was better that he should travel there, even though it would cost him valuable time and money. He didn't want her bumping into Miss Clatworthy. Or Valerie.

Or any of them for that matter.

He returned the letter to his pocket, leaned back in the wrought iron chair, and looked gloomily down into the gently rocking blueness of the water, with its speckles of light and its thousands of floating liver spots.

Even the pool was hung over!

4

On the Monday morning of the week following the receipt of Sofia's letter, Jonty was still depressed.

He was staring through the Staff Room windows, looking out over the drear wet playing fields, wondering if he would always associate this quiet sense of desperation with the beginnings of an English spring in a College for training women how to teach sewing and cooking; and with the heavy scent of snarfia ascending from window-sills carried on currents of dry dusty air disturbed by the central-heating system?

Cheery overtures from Miss Pettigrew, the Botany lecturer, a few moments ago, had done nothing to improve matters. When she had helpfully informed him that the mauve-and-white flora with the long pointed pale-green leaves were 'actually hyacinths', it had somehow increased his sense of desperation.

It wasn't her fault; he HAD been staring at them. And it wasn't only the snarfia-business that depressed him.

It was also the Sofia-business, the teaching-business, the student-business, the Clatworthy-business, the Valerie-business, the Tory government-business, the Common Market-business, the Apartheid-business, and ultimately the One World Government-business.

The insight came upon him that, ever since he could remember, he had sensed a shadowy desperado loitering about his psychological HQ.

Some seasons were worse than others, of course, and he was aware that he would be reaching the final stages of surrender when – the next time he was in Wantage or London (or wherever Sir John Betjeman's tea shop found itself) – he felt ready to drop in for a pot of fresh Twining's, some disturbingly moist crumpet, and a bit of desultory chit-chat on rusty locomotives and defunct railway stations. The question was:

'Am I ready for that NOW?'

He pulled a casual chair as close to the windows as he could, sat down and stared at the drizzle falling on the hockey pitches, as if every drop knew it was signalling the end of something.

The weekend had been as predictably bloody as he had expected.

Most of his time had been spent in deserted rooms on forgotten lines waiting for very slow trains pulling decrepit carriages, and in scanning ancient fly-blown timetables, and in trying to work out routes for going across the country when British Rail had decided, in its bureaucratic wisdom, that passengers should only go up and down it.

This procedure held good for going across to, and coming back from, Birmingham.

And, in between, there had been that detestable and unpredictable meeting with Sofia.

"Why should I provide the evidence? You left ME, remember! And I've now got a bloody respectable job to hold down," said Jonty.

"You – respectable? That's very funny!" snorted Sofia.

"All right. Put it the other way. The respectable job is holding ME down. It is also jumping up and down on my inflamed cuticles and grinning mirthlessly!... Don't let's quibble over details," added Jonty.

"As obscene as ever, I see."

"Of course! A leopard can't change his doucettes, you know."

"What about the divorce?" repeated Sofia.

"Why'd you want it?" countered Jonty. He swept his arm round Crehan's Pad in a wide arc. "You're nicely set up here, aren't you? I couldn't dress you like that! Look at you!"

"Do you want to?" she asked, witheringly.

"Anyway, you can't marry HIM!"

Sofia said nothing.

She looked nearly as marvellous as ever, in an olive-green harem suit that would have cost Jonty several years of salary.

Except that she was thinner. And there were shadows under her eyes.

But, lounging there, in Crehan's Bauhaus chair, her well-known stomach-churning qualities were clearly displayed.

She took another cigarette from a metal case on the glass-topped table and lit up. She drew in a heavy lungful of smoke. It relaxed her.

Jonty's nose wrinkled and twitched as the smoke reached him.

"I've already told you!" she said. "I need money."

"Don't we all?"

"To get it, I need to be free of you. And besides, wouldn't it be better for you?"

"Or for you?"

"I just said so! Since when has your concern been extended to me?" Sofia asked bitterly.

"Oh, it was! It was! But you weren't smoking pot, then."

"Perhaps I should have! You only wanted a good hand with the smalls, the dishes, the feather duster. And, of course, the nightly tumble in the sheets... But I wasn't made to be a skivvy!"

"Oh, I see!" said Jonty huffily. "A gadget you screw on the bed and does the housework, eh?"

"More or less!"

"You've coarsened!" said Jonty.

"From knowing you, I expect!... I'm a painter!" she said vehemently. "Or I'm nothing! This way, the way I want it, I'll be able to paint."

"Are you're sure you're not something else, as well?"

"That's none of your business."

"Who is it, Sofia?"

"That's none of your business, either!"

"Barry?"

She opened her eyes wide and laughed.

"Don't be silly! He's got Alexis."

"Well?"

"He's quite happy with her. And he's no fool."

"So what brings us meeting here?"

"Barry's a friend. Have you forgotten? He just wants to help. It's got to be sorted out, hasn't it?"

"Where'd you get the muggles?"

"Come again?"

"The grass! The dagga! The hemp!"

"Also, none of bloody yours! Why the fuss? You wanted me, but you never loved me, did you?"

The question startled him. He heard again the sound of crying in the rain. Outside his control, a lump fisted up in his throat. He tried to swallow it. 'Oh! "Christ, that my love were in my arms, and I in my bed again." '

The intrusive disturbing images modified his reply:

"Maybe not... I don't know! But I thought I did!"

"You thought wrong... But you've changed, as well, you know."

"Oh? Have I?"

"Yes. You're quieter. More sympathetic."

She laughed: "Listen to us! We've never talked like this before, have we?"

"No, I suppose not!... It took me a solid week to pack up all our things, and clean out Hacking Cough's flat! Why didn't you tell me you were going?"

She laughed again, this time, harshly. "Now, you know what it's like," she said.

"What what's like?"

"There was no point!" She ignored his question. "You had Finals. It would only have upset you."

"You think it didn't?" he asked

"Did it?" she asked in surprise. "Well, if it did, your Finals were over when you realized I'd gone for good."

"I see."

"I don't understand you. You fight everybody. But when somebody fights back, you don't like it, do you? You just don't like the world you live in, that's my belief."

"Wrongo! I love the world. I just don't like the way it crumbles."

"What's the difference?"

"Hard to explain if you can't see it."

"Try!" she said, mockingly.

"What's the point? We live in different sections of it"

"Suit yourself! What about the divorce?"

"You provide the evidence! It's easier for you. I've got a job to keep."

"See what I mean? Full of contradictions. You hate the bloody job! Yet you want to keep it."

"I've got to live."

"There are other ways," she snapped.

"I don't know them!... There is nothing I can do, except teach. And I can't do that. It's got me by the short-and curlies."

"No Arnold Jontys wanted, eh? £6 000 a year! Or was it a month?"

"I'm ready to do it for board and lodging, only! Any takers?"

She laughed again, this time with amusement.

"But I've got my reasons why you should do it!" she said.

"Le coeur a ses raisons, que la raison ne connait point. Hey?"

"What?"

She looked at him through narrowed eyes, suspecting he was making fun of her.

"Pascal!... Tell me!"

"All right! If you must know! I'll give you one damned good reason!"

She thrust out her forearm and pulled back her sleeve. Jonty stared at the small, spreading bruises and the punctures on the meaty part of her arm, near the joint.

"You bloody little fool!" he said, bitterly. "They've got you, all right!"

"Who?"

"All this!"

He looked round the room at the electronic smoothness of Crehan's Pad, at the flick-switch sophistication of it all. It smelled of money. Crehan must still be at it.

"I like it," said Sofia.

"Never give a sucker an even break! W.C. Fields knew a thing or two."

"That drunk!"

Abruptly, he stood up.

He was shocked right down to the soles of his cotton socks. That didn't happen easily to Jonty.

Sofia of all people!

Compared to her poison, beer was a preserver and an elixir of unsurpassable purity. Whereas, she was heading for a country of decay, where everything was negotiable, even down to the formation of the cells in her own body, where randomness would spill its faceless fluids into the smallest crevices of a void that would vanquish all.

Christ! Even the rigid categorical world of Miss Clatworthy was preferable to what Sofia had chosen!

"All right! I'll think about it. See you!" he said, hoping he had kept the disgust out of his voice.

He went out before she could delay him.

She followed him accusingly with her large myopic eyes.

As he closed the porchway door, she was still sprawled in the Bauhaus chair, watching; she did not move, but simply drew on her cigarette until it glowed...

His self-commiserations were interrupted by the squink-squink of composition soles advancing with rapid energy over the linoleum behind him.

He heard the North Country tones of George Upall, subdued in the interests of common decency, but loud enough for Jonty's ears, exhorting him: "Come on, Jonty! Stop thinking about it! Get out there and do it. It's the only way to fight off an early prostate, you know!"

Like Redshins, Upall never stopped thinking about it, even when he was thinking about something else -- unlike Redshins. He was of a similar species, but of the lesser-tufted variety with harsher colouration, a migrant from a more rugged industrial habitat. In fact, he was a fully-mechanized one-piece cock bird with an automatic vibrator and power driven attachments for screwing into and out of things; but mainly in.

He looked after the Art & Craft Department with tireless energy; he was very ambitious and he had set out early to carve an enduring niche for himself, somewhere. He did not mind where he carved it as long as the site of the incision attracted women, money and status – in that order.

Jonty turned to look at him.

"Doing it' is what's caused all the trouble," said Jonty, miserably.

"Don't worry!" said Upall, seating himself in another chair, nearby. "Trouble is just a side-effect. Ripeness is all!"

Jonty noticed for the first time that morning that some of his colleagues had come in while he had been staring into the rain, deep in his introspections.

Doris Crawford, the cat-loving Needlework tutor was also in the Staff Room, tucked into a corner, reading balanced-food advertisements aloud to one of her huge white Persians, asleep on her lap.

Big Rev. Peter Haffler sat in the opposite corner, contemplatively picking his nose and smoothing down his toupee, perhaps working out the next move in the unending chess matches he played by post in every corner of the world. He was a vain and ugly man, both outwardly and inwardly. His ugliness was a continuum from the size of his nose, his fingers and head to the size of his ideas, his prejudices and convictions.

Doris and he were enemies.

He hated cats; she claimed that he sprinkled salt on his shoulders to simulate dandruff.

Secretly, everyone knew he was as bald as an egg.

They went on ignoring each other.

Jonty was glad they were out of earshot.

"I suppose you know," muttered Upall, "that The Pettigrew's been complaining about you?"

Jonty groaned.

"The old hypocrite was as nice as pie to me first thing this morning. She told me what snarfia are called… Not my duffle coat again, is it?

Jonty looked over to where he had seen her near the hyacinths earlier on, but she had gone.

She strutted into his mind, nevertheless, exactly as if she had been there in the flesh: steatopygous, owl-eyed, rictal-bristled either side of her mouth, her complexion looking (as always) as if it was undergoing a short course of keratinization; and dragging behind her his duffle coat, which she was boasting she had just shot fatally in the tripes, with a point three-two at long range.

She was reputed to be a crackshot.

"No. She seems to have dropped that one!" laughed Upall, unconsciously punning on Jonty's musings.

"Bang goes another duffle coat!" said Jonty, still responding to his fantasies.

"Come again!" said Upall.

"How'd you know?" asked Jonty.

"I overheard her talking to Big Rev, just a while ago."

Miss Pettigrew was the College's self-appointed Do-gooder, and she felt it was her duty to keep Big Rev, the professional, informed of what went on in her mind and her life.

No wonder she was a Do-gooder: Jonty believed she had no potential to be anything else. Apart from lacking the capacity to even imagine herself in a wicked situation, Jonty attributed her complexion to the fact that her pores were clogged up with spiritual humility.

After all, a beautiful face depends on the materials you start out with; you can't make it up as you go along, can you, except on the surface?

Like a beautiful soul. They needed beauty of form at the beginning: no amount of cosmetic was much use.

"She was probably giving him the low-down on recent preparations for alopetia, and asking him if he'd come across any new cures for acne," murmured Jonty.

"Not at all, old son. She was telling him how you kept the College Mini out all night. Did you?"

Jonty's stomach flipped: there must be easier ways to get ulcers.

"It's a lie," he said automatically.

George Upall crinkled his forehead at him and smiled sceptically with his teeth.

His out-of-doorsy face was the same shape as a hazel nut, and the same colour, with a lighter patch of hair on top.

"Oh, come off it! You don't have to pretend with me. I saw her yesterday, inspecting it for scratches, outside the library."

"What's it got to do with her?" asked Jonty, indignantly.

"She says she'd booked it for the following morning, at eight o'clock, for a school visit."

"So?"

"She says you didn't arrive in College with it until nine! Bad luck! Who was it?"

"Who was what?"

"Why else would you keep a car out all night? Silly mistake, that!"

He drew air into his mouth, dubiously, between his leaning teeth.

"You could have dumped it in the car park. Late! Nobody would have known. If you want to stage your seductions in the College Mini, for God's sake bring it back in time. Do Minis turn her on, then?"

Jonty ignored Upall's leering expressions.

He was angry with himself: he could so easily have returned it to the car park. But it had been such a filthy night and he hadn't relished walking home, wet to the skin, after all that wonderful, exhausting malarkey with Valerie.

He was also angry with Upall: for guessing the truth of things, one; for pointing out his shortcomings, two; for doing it in his North Country accent, three; for cultivating a Cockney glottal stop, four, (that made him swallow both his tee-and-kay-sounds) to hide his Northern whine.

'If he HAS to say "Bring it back in time" why can't he say "Bring it back in time" instead of "Brin' i' ba' in time"? How does he think he is going to whittle out that social niche with articulation like that?'

"I'll try to be more careful next time, Upall."

"There may not be a nex' time. She's pinderin' abou' trying to ge' the rules changed. Seven a' the la'est! She's but'ering-up Clatworthy, and tha' takes a lo' o' bu'er!"

"The old cow!"

"You wanna watch it! Didn't leave any French Le'ers, under the seat, did you?"

"Bilingual, is she? Knows French?" asked Jonty, innocently.

"Bilingual! She'll be straight up to Auntie Clatworthy's office, translating every clause of your contract to her. You'll be out on your ear – quick as a flash! No collection, no farewell presents, no goodbye ceremony round the eagle on the library spire, with its balls at half-mast because of the sterling service you've pu' in. No fear! I've had some. You watch her! She nearly nailed me, once."

"When was that?"

"Tell you some other time. Above all, leave the students alone. They're jail-bait. And leave the staff alone. Professional virgins, all of 'em!"

The callipygian Pettigrew strutted about in his mind.

"Don't be obscene!" he said, in mock outrage.

"Even the youngest of the virgins have got hymens like Bank grilles. Got to break in with black mask and revolver; and then, it's only for a bag of small change! I know! Take it from me."

"I'm not asking for advice, you know?"

"Take it! It's free, gratis and for nothing. Just being friendly."

"Sorry! I didn't know The Pettigrew was at it."

"Tha's all righ'! She's always a' i' from one direction or another. See ya! Ta-ta!"

Upall rose abruptly and walked away, his legs moving quickly from the waist, his composition soles squeaking energetically on the floor, his trunk stiff and stumpy, his head darting this way and that, jauntily, always searching, a prey to his own predatory instincts, in all seasons, climes and places – the restless, ubiquitous hunter of minge!

'Wonder if I could walk like that? Is he trying to start a trend?'

Jonty looked at the clock at the other end of the room. There had been no recent power-cut: it said, quarter to ten.

He had time to go and pin up a new notice on the board outside the library.

Should he?

Why not?

If Miss Ursula Pettigrew was starting to mobilize the forces of bastardy and march them in his direction, why couldn't he toss over one or two hand grenades of his own? If you can't kill it, harass it: that was the rule.

He got up and went towards the door.

Doris Crawford was still reading softly aloud to her sleeping cat.

As Jonty passed him, Big Rev shuffled his bottom on the velveteen cushions of his armchair and sighted his eyes along his thoughts like a rifle. Jonty expected to feel the impact of the pellet between his shoulder blades as he went out.

Or the bullet.

He felt nothing.

There was a small public road between the Main Building of the College and the library. As Jonty crossed it, he wondered which notice he should remove. He decided it should be the one that said:

IT IS FORBIDDEN FOR THE PRINCIPAL TO THROW STONES AT THIS NOTICE.

BY ORDER.

It had been up for some weeks, and Miss M. Clatworthy had neither thrown stones at it, nor removed it; so its power had probably evaporated, by now.

He decided, therefore, to change his target from a specific to a general one; nevertheless, he hoped it would turn out to be more sensitive to influence than the Principal in person had proved to be, and would, at least, have the advantage of including The Pettigrew within its range.

He looked round the foyer to make sure he wasn't under surveillance himself.

He could see one or two students inside the library, behind the glass windows; but they appeared to be engrossed in their books.

The coast was clear.

He took the paper from his pocket, opened it and smoothed out the wrinkles. He had secretly used one of Upall's thick squirrel-haired paintbrushes and black poster paint to produce it. The letters were a good thumb-length high.

He removed the old notice, made room for the new and larger one by removing some other outdated reminders, and pinned it up so that it would catch the eye as soon as anyone entered the Foyer. It looked good:

WIPE YOUR FEET BEFORE YOU ENTER AND THROW ALL INTEGRITY IN THE RECEPTACLES PROVIDED.

THE PRINCIPAL.

If he was lucky, Miss Clatworthy might give it pride of place on the Agenda of this month's Staff Meeting, instead of the second place an earlier notice had won. That one had read: NO IDEAS ADMITTED TO THIS BUILDING UNLESS ON A LEASH. – THE PRINCIPAL.

On the former occasion, he had been beaten to the tape by the important question of 'Quality of Staff Room Tea', which had come up from behind in the final stages of drafting and won by a head.

Still, second had been better than running with the stragglers at the end of the Agenda on such marginal questions as 'The New 3-Year Revised Syllabus' and 'Welfare Facilities for Sick Students'.

Oh dear, yes!

The more controversial and basic the problem, the less time devoted to its discussion.

That was the First Clatworthy Law.

Fifteen minutes of discussion was the absolute maximum ever known to have been devoted to controversial matters, and even then Miss C. and her Staff seemed to settle them by some kind of telepathic code, marked by nods, grunts and eyebrow raisings that Jonty hadn't been able, so far, to crack, although he had observed it on many occasions at very close quarters.

If this notice got stuffed into the last few items on the next Agenda, or, worse still, did not even get an honourable mention, he'd know his number was up!

Bearing it at all was bad enough; but bearing it without being able to hassle it was unthinkable!

He turned away from the noticeboard.

It was ten-fifteen.

Now, he'd really have to mark those essays on the Metaphysicals!

He breathed in heavily, and prepared himself yet again to pass Miss Clatworthy's door to reach his study.

He squared his shoulders.

"The smell of hyacinths be buggered!" he snorted.

5

"So you see," said Jonty to his father, "what with the Sofia-ballsup, and all the powers of Charity, Enlightenment and Knowledge hallooing in the middle distance, I don't know whether I'm on my arse or my elbow! And now there's the Valerie affair."

"Yes! But it sounds as though you still know where to find the bit that stands up, don't it, son?" asked Tom Godley.

Jonty ignored the question. He didn't feel like taking the discussion in THAT direction, at the moment. So Tom tried another:

"What's the matter with you and Sofia, anyway? I thought you two were fine!"

"Anything but fine! She upped and left me one fine day in Cambridge, and I've seen her only once since then."

"Why?"

"What do you mean – why? How do I know?... I was only her husband," he added woefully.

"What is she after? Has she got a touch of what that Alexis-girl had?"

"Nothing like that!.. She didn't like it when I complained about – about keeping the house clean, and all that sort of crap... She says she just wants to paint."

"Houses?"

"Soup!"

"Oh, she's one of the Arty-Crafty types, is she? Why didn't you let me give her the once-over before you married her, son?"

"Dunno!" he said, then remembered. "Wasn't easy, was it? I was going up to Cambridge, and you were in The Bin."

"Oh, like that, is it?"

"No! I didn't mean it like that! It just didn't work out. I couldn't bring her... Anyway, I wouldn't want her back, now."

"Why not?"

"She's a junkie."

"It's fashionable!"

"Look, Dad! I know how you feel about booze versus goof-balls. We've been over that before. If she wants the jag, she can have it. I don't!"

Tom began to reply, but his son talked him down.

"I know all the arguments! You choose your own way of dying. That's what you say, isn't it? Fine. It's pure Hemingway. But I want to choose my own way of living, too. And I'm not living with THAT."

"All right, all right! So – what now?"

"That's just it. I don't know. What the hell can I do? Just give her the divorce, I suppose. As soon as Aunty Clatworthy hears about it, the entire College will be in uproar. Big Rev will start spewing out puce sermons on the sanctity of family life and marital fornication. The Pettigrew will deride the whole idea of contact between the sexes, with special reference to male tutors teaching female students, and one tutor in particular teaching any woman in general. The place is a sink of virtue. The whole brood will start padlocking themselves into their knickers every morning, and giving out egg-bound clucks every time they see me. The bloody Governors will be called in to discuss the wisdom of employing only eunuchs in future... That, at least, will improve the College choir!... I'll be out on my unmusical ear. If I get a testimonial, it'll only be for some kind of stud-work. And that's IF they don't find out about Valerie. Which eventuality doesn't bear thinking about. 'Howl, howl, howl'!"

"You can always come back with me, son.

"I know. Thanks, Dad. But – me – a bookie! I can't tell a double from a treble. If I'd stayed on with you, they'd have had you in the Courts before you could say 'Shit and derision!'"

"You'd have learnt."

"I don't think I want to learn – not that! It isn't me! "

"What is you?"

"I have never found out."

"Son, I had exactly the same problem! I didn't know who the hell I was until I won this little fortune on the Pools. Then I found out!... It's bleeding wonderful what a bit of luxury does fer your identity... Mind you, it ain't easy, learning to put up with the best of everything. But I manage! Look at me, now!"

He patted the hand-rims of his invalid chair.

"Running on wheels!" he said.

Jonty grinned wryly at his father's joke.

"All that bullshit about poverty and 'ardship moulding the character. It wasn't nothin' to the moulding a bit of the old filthy lucre has managed. Got more character now than I ever had! If money ISN'T character, it's a bloody good substitute!"

And he cackled like an old hen. Godley Senior was happy.

Despite the wheelchair, he dressed well, slept well and worked well.

His father had a desk, a telephone and an office at home, employed several clerks, and had another office in town, which he visited once or twice a week. He rented tiny premises in New Street, next to a Milk Bar. It had a large plate-glass window decorated all over with gaudy scroll-work and curlicues that hid what went on inside. At the top, large bright lettering painted in an arc said:

TURF ACCOUNTANT OFFICE. THOMAS GODLEY (Prop).

He was very proud of it.

Jonty watched the fingers of his father's hands, curled round the rims of the wheels. No longer did they scamper like the little furless animals that used to distress him so much. They were quite still. Nor had he once mentioned Jonty's mother, and the way she died.

Of course, he still drank a lot.

Both father and son agreed that drinking a lot was better than drinking a little.

But for Godley Senior, 'drink' no longer seemed to be a 'devil in solution' that drove and controlled him; only a pleasure that he meted out as required.

At least, that is how, at the moment, it looked to his son.

Jonty rose from the Parker Knoll chair provided for clients.

"Dad, I've got to be off! Sorry! Lots of lectures to prepare."

"Right, son! Right!"

They shook hands across the desk, in the office that had once been a Servants' Pantry.

"When?" asked his father.

"Not sure! Two or three weeks, probably. Whenever the weekend looks free. It's a long trip, you know. Look after yourself. Ciaou!"

"So long!"

At the wrought-iron double gates of his father's new house, Jonty turned and looked back down the driveway, recollecting the first time he had seen it.

It was on his way down from Cambridge, his Finals over, just after his line change at Bletchley.

The Birmingham train had been drawing in to New Street Station when he read again the letter he had found in his suitcase, forgotten, driven out of his head by the antics of the Reverend Newey and Sir Leslie.

Then, in the same buffet where he had once had a conversation with a buttered roll and a bigger-and-tweedier version of Flora Robson, he had read it aloud to a pint of Guinness to make sure he understood it aright.

Winning fortunes, indeed!

On the Football Pools!

Only photographs faked by the Press won the Penny Points and Treble Chance prizes, didn't they? Weren't they inventions of the media, a necessary myth, like the American superstition that any poor man could get to be President of the United States?

Theoretically, the British Working Man – whoever HE was! – had to be able to believe he could (if the opportunity, the place and the luck were right) become a millionaire; his imagination needed such escape-hatches in order to stay alive.

But the odds against actually winning were astronomical; and since when did the Godleys have the odds in their favour?

After his Guinness, Jonty had taken a bus out to the terminus at the Lickey Hills, and walked from there to the hospital. Eventually inside, Jonty was shown to the surgery of the sandy-faced doctor with the ptosic eyelid that he had spoken to four years earlier.

"Good day, Mr Godley."

"Good day, Doctor."

Since Jonty's first meeting with the medic, he seemed to have stepped up the number of urr-urr noises he got into even fairly short sentences. Jonty couldn't help wondering how he would make out on longer utterances.

"Yes, Mr Godley, there is no doubt that he won it. We were all just as sceptical at first as you are. But even before he had this windfall, he had made remarkable progress under this new treatment of ours."

'Windfall!... Stormfall. Miracle!... The Doc seems even better on long sentences!'

"You mean on this gambling lark – urr, thing – urr, treatment?" said Jonty, aloud.

"I beg your pardon!"

The Doctor's expression was a mixture of pain and surprise.

Jonty inferred that he had unwittingly given a competent imitation of the doctor's accent and manner. He would have to watch himself. The urge to try it out had been stronger than he'd realized; but he had no wish to offend the man.

"You mean this gambling faffdangle?" Jonty said again, normally this time.

"I suppose you could describe the treatment in that way!... Faffdangle!"

The doctor repeated it to himself, as if he might be considering incorporating it into his medical terminology for future diagnoses and prescriptions.

"Quite striking!" he said.

'Oh, I dunno! I've—'

"—The treatment, I meant. Almost as soon as we began it, your father improved in leaps and bounds. It proved to be the key to his cure, Mr Godley."

"I bet it did," murmured Jonty.

He could almost hear the tumblers clinking and his father chuckling as he spoke:

'I said to the Doc, what's normal for you ain't normal for me, and what's the betting I'll have a nice little nest-egg in a twelvemonth while you'll still be doing the rounds of all these loonies?'

"What was that, Mr Godley?" asked the doctor, not quite catching Jonty's murmur.

"I'm glad it did."

"So were we all! It's been pleasant to talk to you, and I'm so pleased to be able to tell you that your father is well again. Goodbye, Mr Godley."

Jonty had gone away thoughtful.

As he left the hospital gates, he read his father's address written on the card the doctor had given him: Sharman's Cross, Solihull! God in heaven!

The Executive Belt!

Slap bang in the middle of the stronghold of the Boorgoyzie!

Surely his father hadn't developed aspirations to wearing a collar and tie, had he? What was he going to use for table cloths?... They didn't even read *The Daily Mirror* in those parts... Of course, nobody

CAN in any real sense… you look at the pictures… And as far as The Pink 'Un was concerned – totally out of the question!

These people OWNED the bloody horses!

They didn't need tips about winners. They knew beforehand… You might see a copy of *The Times* or *The Daily Telegraph* or The *Financial Times* – but they would be folded up under somebody's arm, or being read; not opened out and flattened on a table for the china tea-sets to sit on.

It was doubtful if they used crimplene or even damask linen, these days.

A real self-lubricating upper-middle Boorgoyze, with indestructible nylon bearings and a twelve-cylinder Rolls Royce income, would feed off bare English oak or South African yellow-wood; and use gold-lame loo-covers in the johns…

What on earth would his father read in his sober moments at the breakfast table?

Afterwards, Jonty had taken a Midland Red bus out to Solihull to see his parent.

It would be the first occasion he had been able to see him in a long time – since his marriage to Sofia, in fact.

He got off the bus, and began to walk down the wide quiet road where his father now lived.

It was a long walk and there was a lot of space between one house and another.

The residences stood alone in the middle of immense lawns with buried sprinklers green as limes, expensive as emeralds, surrounded by trees that bowed like butlers and curled their leaves in supercilious sighs over the tradesmen's entrances; where even the atmosphere – frisky over the Clean Air Act – pussy-footed about the eaves murmuring 'Yessir, yessir', and politely dusting the H and Y and T-pronged aerials that channelled the very latest Market News to their air-conditioned inhabitants, most of whom had spent their infancies in top or roomy middle-drawers, their clothes fragrant from sachets of expensive herbs, not peppered with little balls of blanket-fluff from under the dresser and smelling of carbolic soap – like Jonty and his father.

The birds whistled courteously among the snarfia and berberis; no raucous twerplings in broad dialects were allowed. Here, Nature was well-watered, properly pruned, carefully subdued, and spoke only in the tones of Received Pronunciation.

From the high to the low, it was the same: modulated frequencies, modulated feelings, modulated greed.

Even the earthworms, Jonty guessed, were worth more from a week's than he from a whole year's work; and when the glistening snooty twerples in their black City suits and bright gold beaks pulled them out of the emerald lawns, they condescended to come with restrained plops only, none of those vulgar squelching noises so beloved of the lumpen proletariat.

It was all so depressingly tasteful, so beautifully unbearable, so luxuriantly sick-making!

The new-minted voters that stepped out of the houses in this area, made even the shenanagins of prime specimens like the Reverend Newey and Sir Leslie look comparatively red- blooded, untidy and virile.

Was the new always actually worse than the old, or did it only seem worse when you compared it with what time had established?

Was there a word, a name, for something worse than the worst, that kept on getting worse?

He must remember to consult the SOD – or should he say in this suburb the Shorter Oxford Dictionary?

Then, Jonty saw his father's house, and he laughed like a sewer in a thunderstorm.

"It ain't funny, mate! I got a bad back!"

So said one of the men in the gang that was busy erecting above the pillared gate of the driveway the largest set of pawnbroker's balls Jonty had ever seen in his life.

Heavy as bathospheres, they swung golden in the sun from a derrick mounted on a lorry; they were being gradually chivvied and cajoled towards a slender, wrought-iron archway that rested atop the pillars, where they would dangle from its apex, flashingly or dully, according to the weather that gentility had allowed into the district for the day.

"Watch the bleeders as they swing back!"

"Look out!"

"You nearly dropped a bollock that time, Arfer."

"Everyfing under control," said Arfer, smug as a bureaucrat, at the levers of the derrick.

Another man, in dabbed and splodgy overalls, was painting a set of letters on a small wooden plate set into the wall, delicately done in the discreet style of the district that said, in utter simplicity:

UNCLE'S.

6

Jonty nodded to the men and stepped onto the gravel of the driveway.

He looked up at the hugeness of the orbs, jubilantly, lightly.

They just couldn't be ignored! Jonty could not have done better himself.

Had his father got any plans to embellish them?

What about a small pot of maidenhair fern suspended in front?

Or, better still, perhaps you could cover them with some kind of chemical compound to encourage the growth of fungus, or even pubic hair?

Had his father thought of that? He would have to ask him.

Jonty turned and walked towards the house, exultingly.

The front door was large; it had a stone portico round it, a mosaic floor in front of it, and a large brass knocker in the shape of a claw screwed onto it.

Jonty lifted it by a talon and let it fall under its own weight.

Inside, there was a boom in a bank vault.

He did it again, several times. Hollowly, the echoing bounced back like a dud cheque.

It made him feel small and immobile; he became one of those alabaster dwarfs that inhabit the gardens of aspiring suburbia.

But, with concentration, he managed to lift his plastercast arm and knock again. This time, he heard a wee goblin voice answering him.

It said: "Push! It's open."

He pushed.

The door opened to reveal his father taxying down a hall the size of a runway in his wheelchair.

"I've come for a job," said Jonty, in his pointed blue hat, his pointed white beard, brown jerkin, and tight scarlet tights. "I'm a dwarf. Conscientious, strong, who'll stand still and unbowed in all weathers. Work for keep only – and free uniform, painted once a year. Not many of us have a BA Cantab, you know!"

"You always was a daft pratt, even as a nipper," said his father. "How are you, anyway? Long time no see."

"I'm fine! How're you?"

"As you see!" he said and smiled.

His father was fatter.

They shook hands.

"Shan't be a minute! I've got some bloke here who's measuring the place up. Have a shifty round, while I talk to him. Back before you can say Jack Robinson!"

And he was gone, his wheels hissing on the marble slabs.

Jonty had no option.

He put down the suitcase he had been carrying since leaving the station – a landing ticket on an empty runway.

All the rooms he inspected were quite big enough for conversion to light-aircraft hangars and quite empty. They had high white ceilings with plaster decorations of snarfia all round the cornices and clumps of leaves collected in their corners: blown there by artistic passion or winter tempests; bas-relief or flood-relief?

'When you design a hangar, do it by the book.'

The window frames were made of stone and as tall as lampposts. The wallpaper seemed to be some kind of fine-textured green sacking.

That was more like it!

The staircase was as big as the A1 motorway, with terraces and marble shoulders to accommodate the blowouts, seize-ups and breakdowns of guests who were accident-prone.

Upstairs was a repetition of downstairs – only more so.

It was ridiculous!

How could his father live here on his tod? He'd pine away with loneliness.

He'd get lost in the Autumn mists on the moors. He might as well rent Stonehenge.

At the very least, he'd get rattled about by March winds, like a seed in a laburnum pod.

What was his father's game? What was he up to?

Jonty stood at the top of the long stretch of stairs and surveyed the length of the hall.

He began to measure it in his mind.

At that moment, Godley Senior zoomed out of a fly-under in the area at the foot of the staircase.

Almost at once, a little man in a flapping white overall came trotting out behind him.

"That just about wraps it up, I think," said Godley Senior.

'In that overall?' thought Jonty.

"Except for the upstairs dimensions, Mr Godley," said the man.

His face was the colour of cigarette ash and his ears stood out almost at right angles to his head, in the shape of cup handles.

A sign of unbridled passion?

But the flapping whiteness of his overall, his complexion and listening equipment gave him the distracted air of an albino bat.

"Don't worry, now!" said Tom Godley. "I'll call you in later to get them."

"Right, then, Mr Godlety! I'll let meself out. Good morning."

And with a quiver of his looped ears, he swept out to gulp down the moths.

Jonty reached the bottom of the stairs and stepped onto the marble floor.

"So, what's all this in aid of?" he asked, stretching out his arms, like an actor trying to embrace an appreciative audience. "All these rooms? All this space? All this emptiness? What's Bat-ears come for?"

"Blowers!" said Tom Godlety.

"Blowers?"

"I'm having half a dozen cubicles built into half a dozen rooms," replied his father.

"Oh! I see! Intercoms for the Flight-Controllers!... From room to room," translated Jonty.

"What should I do that for?" asked Godley Senior, in puzzlement.

"Keep in touch with the servants, I suppose."

"What bloody servants? No servants, here! This is all strictly business. And six or seven long trestle tables. Oh, yes! And some shelves built round the walls. Then we'll be set up. Lovely!"

"Set up for what? Is that all you're going to put in? What about domestic fittings?" asked Jonty, still baffled.

"Don't need nothing else!" answered Tom Godley.

"What? Where's your furniture? Where'd you sleep? How're you going to fill all this?"

"I'm not! You know me. Live in the kitchen. A few old sticks. I'm using one of the built-in cupboards as a bedroom. Beautiful kip! Lovely empty space. Always wanted it. Hate being cramped. Here, I can spread my wings," said his father, "and fly!" He held his arms out like pinions.

"What you want trestles for?" asked Jonty, ignoring him.

"All the racing news. Every daily and weekly paper there is!"

"The shelves?"

"Form Books! Lovely little blue thick things! All round the walls! And pencils. Pads for working out the odds. A few chairs to sit on. And there it is: Big business! I'll be able to move round a treat on these floors. No steps. It'll be as good as having a motorbike. And I've set up my own little office in what used to be the Servants' Pantry. What could be better?"

Before Jonty could reply, somebody started beating a tattoo on the front door.

It made the brass claw sound like a seven-pound demolition hammer. The noise was deafening.

"Push!" yelled Tom Godley. "It's open."

They were both hoping the racket would stop and looked with expectation down the long runway of the hall. The wee goblin voice of Godley Senior must have filtered through to the outside.

The din stopped; the door opened.

It was Arfer.

Heavyfooted, bulky in a thick check lumber-jacket, he walked towards them.

"I fink that's everyfink, Mr Godleyy. They're up!"

Arfer wasn't holding a seven-pound hammer, after all.

"We're buggerink orf, now. Just come to tell you."

"Fanks!" said Jonty.

Arfer, who was about to turn away, stopped, and looked levelly back at Jonty.

"I know there ARE people," said Arfer, with great deliberation, "oo like to make fun of uvver people 'oove got speech 'pediments."

Then he stood watching Jonty, silently weighing him up.

Jonty could hear again in his head, the sound the claw made on the door.

Arfer had done it with his bare hands, without a hammer!

"Oh, do they?" said Jonty, all conciliatory. "They should be ashamed of themselves, shouldn't they?"

"They bleedin' should!" said Arfer.

Arfer stood for a moment considering Godley Junior, came to a conclusion and then looked over at Godley Senior.

"I've left Bert polishink 'em! Mornink, Mr Godley."

"Morning, Arfer."

"Morning," said Jonty, tentatively.

Arfer ignored him.

They watched him walk heavily back down the hall to the door. He opened it, went out, and closed it without a sound.

"Well," said Godley Senior. "That's one thing to be proud of."

"What is?"

"There's nobody in Solihull who's got a garden-gateway as well hung as ours! But one thing we gotta watch for."

"Oh?" said Jonty.

"Mumps! I wouldn't want the bastards swellin'. It could bring the gateway down."

"Don't worry." said his son. "You won't catch it in this stoneless suburb! What are they there for, anyway?"

"Business and pleasure!"

"Business? What business? You'll have to get the Council's say-so to put up signs as big as those. You never know – they might insist on a G-string!"

"I'll worry when they do!"

"But, Pa! Why a pawnbroker's sign?"

"That's what I am! 'Uncle Godley, Pawnbroker'."

"You mean – loans on gold watches and family heirlooms?"

"No fear! Not me! No, the other sort!"

"Didn't know there was another sort! The only kind I know have little grey chin-beards and tell you jokes in Yiddish."

"Didn't teach you much at Cambridge, did they?… Look son! I'm a punter, not a gambler; at least, I only gamble in my spare time. Professionally, I punt... See?… No?… Never mind… But with that big win on the Pools, I got the capital to start the business. Sheer luck! But you can't bank on that. I bet on science – form – knowledge of the tracks – inside info from the jocks – all that stuff! See?... Now, these blokes who'll sit at the blowers will be putting bets on – all day, every day, every race. In THEIR names, but really for me, see? And I'll be putting bets on in MY name for the Big Boys – to cover up for THEM. That's what a pawnbroker is – in racing parlance. A Front Man for the professionals: the Big Boys against the betting firms. Got it?"

"No! Sounds complicated! What happened to your system? Doubling up on all abstract nouns?"

His father laughed heartily.

"That's strictly for amateurs – just a game! All these cubicles – see—?"

He swept an arm through the air, as if they were already installed and visible.

"—These blokes will be getting tips and info from all over the country, see! They feed it to me, and I sift it! I learnt a lot in a short time in the Bin!... I can double my money in no time at all."

"You hope."

"I can."

"We'll see!"

"You'll see. What about a cuppa?

"Good idea!"

His father zoomed away, the wheels of his chair hissing and squeaking across the marble. Jonty followed him, behind the stairway, to the kitchen.

It was as large as the entire house they had lived in before, tall-windowed, high-ceilinged, and fitted out in the best Crehan tradition: a deep-frozen, dry-spun, waste-crushed, melamined, louvred, air-conditioned showpiece.

In addition it had a horsehair sofa, two newish leather armchairs, a television, and several hundred pieces of unwashed crockery in it.

Tom Godley saw his son surveying the piled-up tableware.

"I have a woman in twice a week," said his father, "to clean up."

"Make it twice a day," said Jonty.

"What for?"

"It's too tidy! Let her mess things up a bit, and make it more like home," said Jonty.

"I see what you mean," said his father. "I'll think about it."

Through the stable-top of the huge kitchen door, which was open, Jonty could see a glassed-in verandah.

"What do you keep out there?"

"Plants! You can sleep there, if you like. Makes a good bedroom! Want to stay?"

"Maybe I will! Is there a pot big enough? Does greenfly attack people?"

And that had been the beginning of his postgraduate career as a bookie.

The fact that it hadn't worked out was what had led him, eventually, to a college full of aspiring housecraft teachers.

As no one had, during the period of bookie-ing with his father, specifically advertised to employ Arnold Jonathan Godley for a large salary, nor indeed for any salary, or even for board and lodging, he had started writing around for jobs

He now managed to see his father about once a month, depending on how much preparation for lectures and marking of essays he had to cope with at weekends.

He had just been back on one of his visits.

When he had first seen the driveway of his father's house, it had seemed immense.

Funny, how it had shrunk, how much shorter and narrower it now seemed!

But the pawnbroker's emblems, as conspicuous as ever, still amused him, although they had not grown lichen, had no pubic hair, and were free of crabs.

He now remembered that he had forgotten to ask his father if he had intended to treat them with hair-restorer or growth hormones or antiseptic, and reminded himself to press him on the question next time.

Jonty turned away, a smile on his lips, and began to walk back along Stockbroker's Mall, as he now called it, towards the bus stop.

At this time of the year, the lawns were untidy with winter, gathering their powers, getting ready to unleash their impeccable greens and verniered edges on the winds of March and into the showers of April. The discreet airs were a little less couth than of yore, and the birds a little more ragged, their tones thinner and more tattered.

They'd have to get their acts together if they wished to spend their summers here!

Oh, dear me, yes!

But being a bookie for his father hadn't been too bad in the initial stages.

Sleeping at night in the conservatory, listening to the little snarfia and berberises growing into bigger ones, had been all right; and, in the day, listening to men of various sizes who would never grow again, except fatter, with blowers glued to their ears talking odds, trainers, jockeys, courses, weather, flimps, sachel-men, flyers, staggerers, outsiders, insiders, and dozens of other items he had never heard before, had been fairly all right, too.

It was when Godley Senior had suggested he move to an office in town, as part of his smarter set-up, that things began to be less than all right for Godley Junior.

Even so, he had managed at first.

Receiving the incoming calls from the Big Boys, and phoning the bets out to his father for placement had been easy enough. He just had to be careful that he got the number of noughts right after the digits: these gentlemen didn't use small change.

Occasionally, one of them came in person, with a wad of folding-money so thick it looked like a stage prop. That went straight into the safe. Most of it consisted of waiting.

Jonty had even managed to read some of the books prescribed for him by the Reverend Newey, while he was at Cambridge. He even mused occasionally on whether Newey had stopped the depredations of the beetle in the hammerbeams of Ely Cathedral, or wiped out the fish-rot in his succulents, or leased his lavatory to the Junior Common Room.

What about the book Redshins was writing? What was it called: Sexual Aberrations of Gun Dogs as Depicted in the Religious Verse of the Seventeenth Century? Maybe it was in the bookshops by now?... What had Lady Owens started to collect of late?... And so on... Most of it had been perfectly manageable. Things only began to get out of hand when his father suggested he start a book.

"Start a book? How d'you mean – start one? I've read loads in the last few weeks."

"No, son! I'm talking racing."

And Tom Godley had explained to Arnold about 'round books', 'over-round books' and 'under-round books'. That was the moment that Jonty had felt things were beginning to get on top of him.

"A round book is based on a hundred. See?"

"No!"

"You wangle the odds, so for every hundred quid you pay out you take back one hundred and twenty. It's easy!"

To Jonty, a round book was inconceivable.

A square book, or an oblong book, or a dirty book – yes! Or a good, bad or lousy book.

But a round book whose shape wasn't round: No!

To Jonty, it meant less than nothing. It felt like a dislocation in the Natural Order to even attempt to imagine such a thing. It went against the grain of his education.

He tried.

But when Tom Godley's town office, under his son's management, began giving away large donations to clients, and acting more like the Tom Godley Trust Fund, his father had had to draw the line.

"So that's what your Cambridge education is for, is it? Learned you to read printed books, did it?"

"That's it, Dad! Printed books. Pages with words on. I didn't read for the Mathematics Tripos, you know!"

"Maybe, you should have!"

The upshot of it all was that Godley Senior had employed a pimply-faced young man, named Alf, who was one of the more polished products of a State Secondary Modern School, to take over Jonty's job.

Alf could add up six columns of figures in his head, work out odds on horses while chatting on the blower, smoke a cigarette, gulp hot cocoa, and sit in Jonty's swivel chair, raking it in for his father like a croupier with an eye-shade, ALL AT THE SAME TIME.

Alf said the first thing he had ever read was the Racing Page.

He seemed to understand the enigmas of making books and calculating odds by some mysterious process of absorption through the pores of his skin.

It was one of the rarest moments of stark humiliation that Jonty had ever experienced.

The lash and sting of this exposure drove him to start applying for posts that had something to do with books with words in, which, of course, limited his choice considerably.

No-one could have been more surprised than Jonty, when Miss Clatworthy, after an interview he had assessed as disastrous, sent him a letter offering him the post.

But his acceptance had been the beginning of the end, hadn't it?

Well, they say there's one born every minute!

When was this one's birthday?

7

When Jonty arrived back at St Anne's College, Colchester, on Monday, after visiting his father in Solihull, he had already decided that the point at which Valerie had happened to him was probably going to prove the middle of the end.

Of course, SHE might think that he had happened to her, and he was HER Achilles' heel. It would be grand if neither proved to be a threat and they had happened to each other in the best possible way.

He was hoping so.

Could the cliché be right – 'something bigger than both of them' had happened after all? Would he be able to escape the clichés for ever?

Not knowing was often much better than knowing, wasn't it?

Jonty sat alone in the odour of hyacinths in the Staff Room, musing about the glutinous material he seemed to be squelching through for most of his diurnal round.

This particular formulation of the problem pleased him. His choice of imagery and vocabulary seemed to compensate in some odd way for the conditions underfoot, which got stickier, deeper and more evil-smelling by the day.

Certain events, robust, hairy and sweaty, had grabbed hold of large shovels and started heaving one or two extra tons of the stuff right onto his path; and others had lately dug treacherous potholes in the most unlikely spots for his feet.

For instance, only last month, Norman Upall had come into the Staff Room with his trend-setting walk and started to lament the severe shortage of elastic-sided vaginas in the teaching profession – totally unaware of the inelastic Ursula Pettigrew pinning up another poster about the inflexibility of the United Nations, hidden by the alcove that held the bullheaded Staff Notice Board.

Jonty had gone rigid with embarrassment.

"Sexual starvation is my trouble," said Upall, loudly. "It lowers my intellectual efficiency. It's the one thing I had in common with President Kennedy. Another stiff bout of constupration is called for. The question is – who?"

"Shhh!" Jonty made agonised faces. "Ursula!"

He whispered, jabbing the air with his index finger, indicating a place behind Upall's shoulders.

"Ursula!" yelped Upall, in surprise. "What makes you think I'd even contemplate putting—" he had replied before the danger of the situation struck him. "Oh, no!" groaned Upall.

He whipped round, horrified at his *faux pas*. But it was with relief that he turned jauntily back.

"Don't worry! She won't hear across there."

"Don't you believe it! She's equipped with a special radar for this sort of thing."

"Anyway, she won't know what constupration means."

"Shhh! Don't say it again, man! There's dictionaries! Look at the expression on her face!"

"She can't help that. It's due to the physiology of her beliefs. Too tight under the groin!"

Jonty shook his head and again shushed urgently at Upall, who switched quickly to discussing the end-of-term arrangements as

Ursula, in deep silence, passed them on her way to a lecture; but it was not as deep as she would have wished, on account of the heaviness of her legs and feet. Her face dramatically indicated that she was in acute pain…

After this event, Jonty felt sure that she had placed him high in her Children of Darkness League, a private game she played in cahoots with Big Rev; they made sure that the names were the currency of common gossip from week to week.

However, he didn't mind all that much, as his name had appeared since in between those of D.H. Lawrence and Brendan Behan.

Later, she had made Jonty one or two offers of reconciliation or – more accurately – peaceful coexistence; for Ursula Pettigrew's proffering of the friendly hand was characteristically experienced by most people as a Karate chop to the breadbasket.

Jonty charitably felt, however, that she couldn't be blamed; after all, genetic factors were against her, and her kindest performances often looked like studied insults.

For example, her bad complexion and protuberant behind together changed a near insult into an utter affront; and these two properties coupled to the monotony of her voice, her unvarying pace, her lack of warmth, her near absence of thought and the general use to which she put the English Language, nearly always raised an utter affront to the power of a preposterous insult.

Furthermore, everything that belonged to the entity dubbed Ursula Pettigrew was clothed in sombre, one-toned religious hues that gave her the look of a badly written and produced tract, and made Jonty want to tear her up at once and throw her into a wastepaper basket.

One of her offers of *détente* had come on a day that seemed to have been egregiously filled with unadulterated bastardy.

She had cornered him at the end of a corridor after he had just given four lectures on the trot to two compellingly obtuse Housecraft Groups, who were all taken up with writing theses on ready-made cake-mixes and eye-level grillers, and who couldn't have cared less about the subject of Jonty's lectures – Secondary Modern School Method – on which he knew little, anyway, and had prepared almost nothing besides.

However, it had left him disgruntled, and with few reserves to withstand being addressed like the tail-end of a Vestry Meeting by The Pettigrew.

"Oh, Mr Godley, I've been wondering when I'd see you again. You don't seem to put in very regular appearances! But I suppose that must be my – my—"

She gave up this line of innuendo and followed another. "Are you doing anything right now, Mr Godley?"

'If you go on like that,' thought Jonty, 'I may very well be doing something now, and doing it all over you.'

Jonty saw her owl-eyes fixed predatorily upon him and decided to reply with as much restraint as he could muster.

"Doing anything, Miss Pettigrew? Not unless you call feeling tired, doing something. But I was just—"

"—Would you like to come to tea, Mr Godley?"

"With you!"

"Of course, with me!... It isn't nice to raise your voice in that fashion, Mr Godley. How strange you are!"

Two sets of bristles quivered menacingly at each side of her mouth.

'What fashion?'

Jonty had been taken by surprise and rocked back on his heels by her counter-punching. First, an invitation, and then an admonition.

'Does she mean: "Don't speak to me louder than you usually speak"? Or: "Don't speak in a screech"?

Either way, an invitation to tea with The Pettigrew at the end of even a good day is a lousy trick to pull. I'd rather drown ignominiously in gum boots in a swimming bath of best bitter than come and—'

"—I've got a spoonful or two of home-made jam in the bottom of the pot. I was about to throw it out—"

'—Goddam it! Don't half-rhyme things!—'

"—It's plum! I don't think it's quite off, yet. We could go along in my car. It would be a shame to throw it away if I can put it to good use by asking—... I've had so much of it, you know!"

'So she thinks I'm a mobile dustbin, does she? Make her conscience feel better, do I? Or maybe she's short of jars and wants to wash it out for a new batch?'

"Well, I'm awfully sorry," said Jonty aloud, "but plum jam makes me break out in boils. Must be an allergy!"

"Oh, does it? What a pity! I'll just have to throw it away, I suppose. Maybe another time, Mr Godley?"

'I shall be suffering from carbuncles next time, great big purple ones with crusts on them like cottage loaves.'

"We must hope, Miss Pettigrew, mustn't we? Thank you," he said aloud.

"Not at all, Mr Godley!" said The Pettigrew, and she shook her head.

'I wish I could do that with MY moustache,' thought Jonty. '...Let her collar Big Rev! Let him suck the spongeful of vinegar!'

She strutted off, heavily.

Jonty imagined that The Pettigrew's parting words, characteristically double-edged, to a series of visitors sated on spoonfuls of crystalline, slightly fermented plum jam and a squeeze of vinegar, also homemade, would probably follow the pattern of: "Would you like to take these flowers home with you? They aren't quite done, yet! I've just bought myself some more."

Jonty felt he had made another plunge down the League Table of the Children of Darkness as soon as he had seen her mouth tighten at his refusal.

Whose name would be next to his now? Lady Faulkner? James Callaghan?...

'Well – would she fancy a body full of boils as the price of "being nice"?... Don't worry, Ursula, I've got more allergies than you've got used-up pots of jam!... I should have told her that all sweet foods bring me out in the King's Evil. Her love of Royalty and her disapproval of me might have produced an interesting form of schizophrenia.'

Jonty felt it was burden enough trying to avoid meeting Valerie in the open corridors, whom he liked a lot, without also trying to prevent himself falling over The Royalist Pettigrew, whom he didn't like at all.

Anyway, sharing a spoon of granulous plum jam with HER held no thrill of any kind for him. It wasn't even as if she had invited him to a full jar of shop-jam, stuffed with chemical colouring and preservatives though it may have been!

But a preservative made with her own unfair hands in her own home and nearly fizzing!

Insupportable!

Not only that, Doctor Lovingood and the Reverend Newey at Cambridge had put Jonty off afternoon teas, as a genre, for ever and ever, A-men!

Jonty took a large lungful of the scent of hyacinths and went on with his musing. He would probably keep the Staff Room to himself until Morning Break. Most tutors preferred to discharge their lectures early and have the rest of the day unimpeded.

Although Jonty was out of bed and put in an appearance at the beginning of the timetable with the rest of them, he didn't actually wake up until midday, and thus preferred his mornings free.

These periods of musing helped him, also, to realize where and who he was: the first of which was much easier than the second.

He knew that the latter would take him an undefined and unspecifiable period of time to achieve. He had even faced the prospect that he might never accomplish it, and he preferred facing that in the Staff Room to confronting it in his study, because he would have had to pass Clatworthy's eyrie to get there.

Jonty lived in quiet terror of the days when he had to lecture to Valerie's group.

Knowing that she was there, sitting among the other students, did disastrous things to his thought-processes. It diluted them to a quality roughly equivalent to those dished-up by the Embroidery group in their essays on the subtleties of Tennesee Williams's stagecraft. He only had to look up from his notes and see her sitting there, blonde, small and incredibly bedworthy, for his mind to act like the inside of an oven whose door had been suddenly opened in the middle of a crucial baking session: his ideas, a ruined cake, sank in the middle immediately.

At other times, they felt as if his Needlework group had truncated them with the largest pair of crimping shears they could find, so that they came out in four drop lengths: short, very short, ludicrous and frayed.

It was terrible.

He wanted to wrap himself up in some of the longest pieces available, like a mummy, and die.

But, always, his second reaction was a little more cautious: for example, to feel that the weather was probably getting a little too warm for bandages and, anyway, who was competent in embalming?

It would probably turn out to be The Pettigrew, charitable as a funeral – so put like that, it was decidedly better to remain vertical and try to go on speaking, wasn't it?

Even a full lecture was only fifty-five minutes, after all!

Nonetheless, whenever he could contrive a meeting that looked natural, he saw Valerie.

And whenever she could manage to do so, she saw him. Perhaps it would be for a minute or two in the foyer of the library; or in front of a notice board; or wherever.

It was little enough, but it was the biggest compensation he had.

Another was the steady progress of his war against the forces of bastardy: his communiqués and reports from the front continued to arouse satisfyingly indignant responses from the Principal's eyrie, as well as consistently outraged halloos in Staff Meetings. Their reactions also brought home to Jonty the extent of the powers of survival and self-renewal he had to contend with in the conflict.

During their last Staff Meeting, therefore, he had emphasized to himself the continuing need for guerrilla activities.

The third of his compensations was Doris Crawford. She was regarded as eccentric by her colleagues, and mavericked.

Thus, apart from the minge-hunting Upall, she was the only tutor in the College that Jonty could talk to without being made forcefully aware of the length of his hair, the inadmissibility of his ideas, and the fact that his maleness alone was a threat to the purity and safety of the establishment.

At first, Jonty had wondered why Doris Crawford was discreetly but firmly ostracised. Her appearance was thoroughly conventional and, on the whole, she was not loud or conspicuous in manner or speech.

Jonty discovered later, however, that she did have her own mind and her own view of things, which often ran counter to the orthodoxy that prevailed in the College at the time.

For instance, she said objectionable things in Staff Meetings, such as: "I'm afraid I can't agree with that!"

Or distasteful things like: "Could we have more information on that point?"

Or things interpreted to be subtly subversive, like: "Individuality in students is a good thing to encourage, don't you think?"

She had even been known to make excuses on their behalf such as:

"They're in a learning situation. They're bound to make mistakes!"

She was deemed to be a very cross-grained person indeed.

Furthermore, strictly against Miss Clatworthy's prohibition to have them in College at all, she sometimes brought her cats to the Staff Meetings. As a consequence, in one session the Principal had touched delicately upon the propensity certain animals had to become anti-social when trying to satisfy their natural needs; so Doris had accommodated her Superior's objection by putting down an earth-tray in one of the store cupboards of the Needlework Department, where she worked, and made sure they used it before bringing them to the Staff Meetings.

The Persians didn't mind this in the least, as the store cupboard provided a leg-up from their usual facilities, which were the backseat and rear window ledge of her Vauxhall Victor.

In any case, they provided a welcome diversion to Jonty.

The Persians were more alert than most of his colleagues at these meetings, which they illustrated, while the majority dozed, by maiowing derisively at crucial points in marathon discussions on boring topics like: 'Should the College insist on short hair, long assignments and the wearing of uniforms?'

Also, the Persians travelled a lot.

Doris Crawford claimed they had all done 30,000 miles in one year – and on only forty-four air fresheners and one set of tyres!

Jonty enjoyed listening to her going on about her cats.

"I won't send my Persians to a cat's home, anymore!"

"No? Why not?"

"Last time, they put one of them in a rabbit hutch, and it came back full of fleas. When I go to a hotel, do you know what I tell them? I say, 'If you don't have me, you don't have my cats!' I combed the fleas out and dropped them from the car window."

"Where?"

"Some in Cumberland and some in King's Lynn."

That's the way she held her conversations. They were portmanteau: she talked about several things at once. Verbally, she took a porter and six trunks when she could have got her essential luggage into a small case.

This oddity went along with her incisiveness in Staff Meetings, when, if she wished, she could go to the heart of things with one of her impolite but well-placed questions.

Her own witticism about Cumberland had amused her a lot and Jonty watched Doris Crawford laughing her laugh.

It was a succession of glottal stops, fed by a pulmonary air-stream. Jonty imagined it bubbled up the way a hot-spring, in New Zealand, came forth, but without steam, and of doubtful curative properties, although it seemed to do her a lot of good.

She was a rather big-boned, rectangular woman, with straight grey hair, protuberant eyes, and brogues.

All her movements were quick and jerky – as if her joints stuck at certain points and needed oiling.

How she produced such delicate paintings was a mystery: you'd have expected them done with barbed wire on smeared glass.

But, nothing of the sort!

Large impressive canvases, full of detail, smoothly and beautifully executed.

But her laugh was jerky!

Upall told him that, before Persians, it had been Samoys and Pugs.

College opinion had been so strongly consolidated against the dogs that even Doris Crawford had had to give in and had finally got rid of them.

He said, in winter, she had used to exercise them in the College hothouses. Doris claimed the air coming off the estuary of the River Colne was too cold for them and so she bathed their paws in Irish Whiskey (which is triple-distilled and spelt with the '-e-') and wrapped them up in scarves and blankets and – on their birthdays – baked cakes for them in the local kennel colours.

Afterwards, the Head Gardener said that the greenhouses had become so malodorous he had had to stuff his nostrils up with camphor; so that his most prized snarfia tended to curl their leaves and wilt; and that those in pots on the floor had given up the ghost completely.

It was for reasons like these that Jonty easily forgave Doris Crawford for belonging to the resident troupe of lifelong spinsters he worked with; but he felt it had been a terrible waste of Irish Whiskey, nevertheless.

"My agreement ended last week," she said, rubbing her big hands up and down the skirt of her heavy blue tweed suit.

'Yasus!' thought Jonty. 'I do wish she wouldn't sit with her knees open!'

"You're retiring?" he asked.

"Retiring! Gawd, no! I mean my flat. So I went to my landlord and asked him: 'What do I do now?' He said: 'Carry on.' So I'm carrying on. I've had a row with a different neighbour every day so far."

Her hot-spring laugh started up again.

"What will you do when you run out of neighbours?" asked Jonty.

"Move to another flat, I suppose."

He expected her to allow her laughter to begin bubbling out once more, but she was silent.

Instead, she looked up at him with her bulbous eyes and then down at her skirt again, quickly.

Is she going to try selling me a cat; or to start a rumour about Big Rev?

But what she said was far worse.

"I hope you don't mind my mentioning this—," she began, and stopped.

Jonty felt that another millimetre of his stomach tissue had set out on its journey towards ulceration.

"What?" he asked, apprehensively.

"Haven't said it yet! Patience is a virtue, possess it if you can… It's all these old biddies in the battery. They're clucking again!"

"Well, that's what they're for – clucking!"

"I know. But it's not about me, this time. It's you!"

"What have I done?"

What he had done flashed only too vividly before his eyes.

But feigned ignorance seemed to be a step nearer to real innocence than false denial.

She jerked up her head and looked slyly across to where Big Rev was sitting in his chair, contemplating the board of his mind laid out in black and white squares. A small involuntary twitch of his hand revealed that he was moving a knight to Q7, or a queen to K5.

'A funny paradox,' thought Jonty, 'Big Rev being so fond of chess. It's one of the few games you can't cheat at.'

Big Rev was quite engrossed.

Jonty looked back at Doris Crawford.

'Oh, Yasus! Open wider. Thank you. It's not what you show, it's the way that you show it. Close, and wash out in the basin, please! That's right!'

She began again:

"It's bruited around that you've been seen out with one of our problem students."

"There's no law against it!"

"That's what you think! There's a law against nearly everything in this place, from cats to sex. You seem to be on the sex-end of the spectrum."

'Pussies at both ends of it, hey? So Doris Crawford and I have more in common than I thought!'

"What are they saying?" he asked aloud.

"The worst! It's because you're married. As a single man, they could have done nothing. But bachelors are not allowed in, anyway!"

"Heads I win, tails you lose!"

"Of course! The purity of the battery must be preserved at all costs… It's been passed right down the pecking order, you know? Or rather, right up AND down. It started in the middle!"

"I can guess who."

"Who?"

"She's got a fungoidal complexion."

"On the button! Besides – she's such an awful knitter! I think you'd better be careful."

"Thanks for the warning! I will."

"Pleasure!"

And she got up and went.

That encounter had occurred last Friday, just before he had left for his weekend visit to his father.

First, Upall! Now, Doris Crawford had warned him, too!

General Clatworthy's Commandos for Chastity and Public Ordure must be closing in to take up their assault positions…

Jonty stretched himself in his chair. He was beginning to wake up.

The smell of hyacinths had lessened slightly. The clock said a quarter to eleven. It wouldn't be long now before they began to drift in to the Battery for their tea-and-mash break.

He supposed he had better switch on the kettle, as was customary for anyone there at the time.

No sense in antagonising them needlessly, was there?

Languidly, he rose and went across to the table, set with its battalion of cups and saucers.

You could tell where you were, even if you didn't know, couldn't you?

If so, it was a clear call to assume the prone position for heavy drinking tonight, as soon as possible.

'And I hereby resolve to heed the call.'

8

He couldn't bear it any longer.

A few days later, although it was strictly against their agreement, Jonty decided to ask Valerie to visit him at his flat.

As a third year student, she was allowed to find accommodation outside College, and she had jumped at the chance. She rented rooms not far from the large old house where Jonty lived in a district that had once been very grand, built at one of the highest points of Colchester town. An air of distinction still attached itself to the residences in the area, but it was beginning to feel uncomfortable and she had considered removing elsewhere.

Not being certain she should have accepted Jonty's invitation at all, she approached the stone-framed front door of 5 Griffield Road with some trepidation.

She was confronted by a huge goitre-faced brass-necked lion's head that slept deeply with a thick ring through its ears and its breath heavy with metal polish.

Valerie looked at it dubiously. It had a stick-on label beside it, the size of an envelope, that said: PLEASE DO NOT ANNOY LEO. USE THE BELL.

Valerie was very willing to comply.

But where was it?

She scanned the green-painted panels of the door. She looked at the brightly polished brass knob, near to her right hand. She looked at the iron Victorian boot-scraper at her left foot.

She looked upwards.

The door stretched high above her, but there was nothing like a bell-push to be seen anywhere. All she could see was an inch of plaited wire poking outwards through a hole at her right hand, in the door jamb.

Could that, by any chance, be the bell?

She grasped it between finger and thumb and gave it a good jerk. She was immediately answered by the muffled tinklings of small bells, deep in the innards of the house.

Why didn't the landlord announce it with another small label that said: BELL?

Valerie waited.

In a moment or so she heard the clopping of heels on stone flags approaching her; then the opening of a vestibule door; and, finally, the outside door was opened, too.

Valerie stood before Jonty in the fullness of her being: blonde hair, acorn-cup hat, golden wool sweater, ocean green skirt, black stiletto shoes, and a little anxiety.

"Hullo!" he said.

"Oh, it's you! H-hullo," she replied, hesitantly. "What a posh house! How many storeys? And that knocker!"

"Yes. Mr Bennet comes up every Sunday morning to polish Leo!" said Jonty.

"Mr Bennet?"

"The landlord… But wait till you see inside," he added. "You won't think it's posh, then!"

She stood on the step, miserably, hesitating to enter.

"Oof!" exclaimed Jonty. "Aren't you glad to see me? Aren't you going to come in? What a sour puss!... What's the matter?"

"We agreed not to! Suppose somebody sees me?"

"I know! But I couldn't stand any more of it. Too much bastardy! Not enough beer! Too much work! Not enough—"

"Not enough what?" she asked.

"I wanted very much to kiss you," said Jonty.

"Well! I suppose I'd better come in, then," she said, matter-of-factly.

Jonty closed the heavy wood-panelled door behind him, and the sun went out.

"Oooh! Isn't it dark?" she said.

"I like vestibules when they're as dark as this."

Valerie said nothing, but she clasped him about the waist with both arms and snuggled her body up against him, her shoulders under his armpits.

"Now, you can!" she said.

So Jonty did.

At first, he was very surprised to find that he wasn't as interested in her as he thought he had been.

Why?

Had he been seriously jaded by the forces of bastardy? Had they insidiously sapped his vital energies?

However, the compactness of her body next to his was very nice, and the longer he went on holding her, the more it improved.

He kissed her again.

Her mouth was soft, but not too soft, and she tasted good.

Yes, it was nicer than he'd remembered – like that early spring morning he had once experienced, unexpectedly, on the Malvern Hills (although, as a general rule, things of the early morning were not nice).

Valerie began to respond to his kissing by wriggling her body closer to him, and he began to respond to her responses.

Something was struggling out of a dark place inside him, pricking up its ears, and beginning to look around. The longer they went on canoodling, the more alert it got. He felt that the day, also, had begun to wake up – and not before time, either, because it was five o'clock in the evening.

His mouth was now pressed firmly against hers.

She began to struggle.

"Mmrtrnrn!" she said.

He lifted his head to allow her to speak.

"Talking with your mouth full!" he said.

"Whoo!" she said. "I can't breathe. You were suffocating me!"

"Was I? Sorry! I couldn't see; it's dark."

'That's quite a performance for a man who thought he was indifferent, isn't it?' thought Jonty, realizing the speciousness of his reply.

He released her.

She turned and went through the vestibule door into the large gloomy hallway.

Jonty followed her.

In front of them was a wide marble staircase: shades of 'Uncle's', only much seedier.

"Where does that go to?"

"Upstairs!" replied Jonty.

"Oh, clever, very clever! I mean, what's up there?"

"On the first floor, there's a Commercial Traveller... a waitress... and, oh yes, a mausoleum!" said Jonty.

"A what!"

"I'll show you, later. And, up above them, a lot of other people. I'm not sure who. Never met them."

"Is this yours as well?" asked Valerie, nodding to a door in the hallway that stood to the left of the staircase.

"Yes."

"Oh, let me see!"

"There's nothing in it," said Jonty. "Only an old blue velvet curtain on a string over the window."

She opened the door and peeped in.

"The ceilings are such a long way off. It's so big!"

"Come!" said Jonty. "Follow me. I live in the kitchen."

He passed between the staircase and the doorway, where there was a small passageway leading from the hallway to the kitchen behind.

At the bottom of the passage was a door, which he opened.

He went in, but Valerie stood in the doorway, looking round. She was silent for some time, then she said: "Yes. I see what you mean! The lion misleads you, doesn't it?"

"Leo is a fraud! The whole building is a fraud. I call it Bennet's Folly. Fastening Leo there is like fixing a bow-tie on a turd. But I like it! And once you're in that hall, it's got no pretensions at all, and that's a bloody change, in this world."

"My! We are bitter and twisted today, aren't we?"

"Not especially. Condition normal… Anyway, let me look at you!"

Valerie twirled about in the accepted manner, modelling her outfit.

Under the high-crowned blue hat, shaped like an acorn cup, her long hair sprayed out over her shoulders in a honey-coloured exfoliation of light.

"Marvellous! Your colour exactly!"

"Thank you, sir," she said.

The skirt fell back to just below her knees and the long wool sweater stayed low on her hips, making them appear rounder than usual.

Valerie's sexiness was different from Sofia's.

Sofia's had been ripe, full of juice, dark, stomach-churning.

Valerie's was a semi-abstract picture: subtly-related colouring, the craftsmanship sheer and deft, the composition satisfying, a joy to behold.

He could gaze at her without the animal in him getting up at once to growl and prowl, frightening away gentler feelings.

Of course, if he gazed too long, it would get a little restless, start sniffing the air and, eventually, growl. But the tones were more subdued, and deeper, more affectionate.

"What do you call this colour?" he asked, touching her hat with a fingertip.

"Kingfisher blue. It's all the rage! Do you like it?"

"It was invented for you!.. The outfit must have cost."

"Not much!... I made it," she added proudly.

"You didn't!" Jonty was open-mouthed with admiration.

"Well, I'm not a student at a Housecraft and Needlework College for nothing, am I?"

"I'll say you're not!" said Jonty, with enthusiasm.

"Pat Higgs helped me."

"You mean that girl with the doopers and the rich dad! The 'what-she wears-today-is-in-Vogue-tomorrow' girl?"

"That's her! She's a wiz on clothes. She cut out all the patterns and I sewed them. I'm glad I spent the time making them. Now, it's been worth it!"

"You've been holding out on me! Refusing to come out! All that cock-and-bull stuff about assignments, *et cetera.*"

"Not entirely! I thought it safer that way."

"Yes, you're right, of course! Doris Crawford alerted me that The Pettigrew is scratching around, again. Upall warned about the same thing, earlier."

"Rumours are going the rounds in the dorms, too… But Upall is no saint. We are all wary of Mr Upall!"

"So you should be! He tells me he peels his end in a fresh batch every year."

"I know! He asks girls to pose for him… But he's quite a good sculptor, really."

"Oh, so that's how he does it, is it?" mused Jonty.

"Why did you look so downcast when you came to the door?" asked Valerie, apparently changing the subject.

"Did I?"

"Yes, you did!... These rumours worrying you?"

"Partly. Other things, too."

"What?"

"Look! Let's have another beer, first, shall we?"

"Another?" she asked, playfully.

"Another for me, I mean! I'm afraid to ask you to sit down in this – this mess. You look so unsullied."

He swung his arm down the long, narrow, high-ceilinged kitchen.

She smiled. "There'll be somewhere," she said.

"Look at it!" he said, in mock misery.

There was a door at both ends: the one they had just entered, and the other led to the scullery beyond. At the scullery-end was an old iron stove, the chimney-pipe of which went palsiedly up through the ceiling. A long, wooden scrubbed-top table – that had rarely been scrubbed – ran the length of a wall on the left, whose colour and texture resembled over-cooked poached eggs.

Valerie thought it most distasteful.

In the middle of the wall on the right was another door, with flaking paint, which was seemingly never opened.

"What on earth have you done to the walls?" she asked with a grimace.

"Done to them! You should have seen them when I first came. Somebody had enlarged old leprosy maps and used them as murals! And the lumps looked as if they might be getting ready to suppurate and—"

"—Oh, you make it sound horrible!"

"—So I distempered them in that yellow colour. But it's gone all white round the lumps! Bacteria, I suppose," he added, sorrowfully.

Valerie shuddered.

"Mr Bennet thought it a great improvement when he first saw it. 'Like sunlight pasted on the walls,' he said... Want to come into the kitchen?"

"What for?" asked Valerie, nervously, taking a step through the doorframe.

"It's my private aquarium of silver-fish!" said Jonty, weirdly.

"Oooooh! Yacky!" Valerie shivered. "How can you bear to live here? Yacky, yacky, yacky!"

"It's an adventure!... Anyway, it's all I can afford, at the moment. What about a beer?" asked Jonty, indicating their location.

"Out of that scullery? Is it disgusting?"

"Yes! But the beer's in bottles and it's cool in there. It must be, or the snails wouldn't like it."

"Oooh, yack! It's terrible! You can't eat food out of place like that."

"Who does? I use it for shaving in."

"Why don't you shave in the bathroom?"

"The scullery's prettier! All those little shiny trails!"

"Is it that bad, too? Oh dear!"

She sighed, deeply. Her distaste expressed itself in the stance of her whole body.

Jonty felt sorry about it, but could do nothing to put it right, except to fetch the beer.

9

He brought back two bottles and a clean glass. He put them on the long table, beside the glass already there, half full, of his earlier snort.

"Where did you find that tumbler?" Valerie asked, doubtfully.

"It's quite clean. Honest! There's actually a very good fridge in there."

"Arnold, you're a liar!... Is there?"

"No! But it's okay. Really!"

He poured out her beer, keeping the froth to a minimum

"When it rains is the worst... Well, I'll tell you! In the last storm, I was sitting here minding my own business, when it started to drip through the ceiling in a steady-looking stream. One there, and one out there."

He pointed to a patch in the middle of the composition floor of the kitchen, and another outside in the passageway.

"Put a bowl under one and a bucket under the other. And you know what?"

"No! What?"

"The water stained them… Both… Black… I had to scrub them to get them clean."

"How?"

"With soap and a hard brush!"

"No! I mean, why black?"

"Pitch!"

"How do you mean?"

"Tar! It's on the roofs."

"But – I thought you said there are two more floors above you?"

"I did! At first, I thought somebody had forgotten to turn off a tap in the bathroom… It wasn't!… It was rain. I found out later that behind the façade of gables, the roofs of this building are flat. And there's an intricate system of cracks that lets it through to each floor… Until it reaches mine, at the bottom."

"You don't mean—?"

"—I do!"

"Why don't the other tenants catch it first? In buckets?"

"Don't ask me! Easier to let it soak through, I suppose."

"But that's terrible!"

"They know I can empty it out in the garden. They can't!… There was one leak I couldn't locate for a long time. But I found it, in the end… In there!"

Jonty nodded to the flaking door on the right-hand wall that Valerie had assumed was never opened.

Her expression was apprehensive.

"What's in there?" she asked nervously.

"Thought you'd never ask!"

"Arnold! You're not going to show me something horrible, are you?"

"Depends how you look at it!... It was nailed up. Had a devil of a job to get it open. But it was worth it."

Jonty strode over to the door and suddenly yanked it wide open.

"Look!" he said.

Valerie gave a horrified little scream and put her fist in her mouth.

It was a small cupboard-like room without windows, perhaps a disused broom-store.

Growing out of the floor up to the ceiling were delicately pale and sinewy liana-like plants, with tendrils sprouting from them. On the walls was a medley of different coloured moulds, in various stages of luxuriance: blue, mauve, olive green, and yellow ochre: pebbles, bubbles and rocky lumps of it. Flat drier patches of fungi dotted the walls and floor in between the swellings of mould.

The entire cupboard exuded the smells of reeking tropical jungles and hot steaming forests.

"Oh, shut it up, for God's sake!" screamed Valerie. "I can't bear it!"

"No wonder it was nailed up, hey? Quite a find, really. We shall have to tell The Pettigrew. She can bring her Biology Group to do some Field Study here!"

Jonty closed the door.

Valerie visibly relaxed. She took a large gulp of her beer.

"Oh, Arnold!" she said, as if commiserating over some enormous tragedy. "Why do you live here?"

"Quite a place, isn't it?" he asked proudly. "I like it!... All for a couple of quid a week!"

"But how can you?"

"Easy! It's real! It's earnest! It's cheap! Leaves me more beer-money at the end of the month... Anyway – it's so disreputable around here, I'm not likely to see any of the bloody old frights I work with, am I?"

"Yes! Well! There's always that," said Valerie, with heartfelt sympathy.

"AND I get exercise! Opening that door, for example; and emptying out the tar-water over next-door's fence and taking the spiders out for walks."

"Oh, yacky! You're a terrible man! Really! I don't know why I like you so much." She mused. "Why do I?... I suppose it's because you're different."

"Am I?... Well, it's not everybody who has got two heads, is it?"

"What else is worrying you?" she asked, taking him off-guard.

'There goes one of these feminine leaps again! Right over the water-jump.'

Jonty then told her about Sofia's demand for a divorce.

"Well – give her one!"

"It's not as easy as that."

"Why not?... Of course, if you still want her, there's nothing to be said, is there?"

"Now, don't start getting huffy! I didn't say that."

"I'm sorry!" she said, and smiled at him, radiantly.

The light of it went straight into his occipital lobes and blinded him. It wasn't the first time she had done that, and he hoped it wouldn't be the last.

"Don't smile!" he said. "It disorganizes my thought processes... You don't understand. She wants evidence. And evidence of you-know-what! And that means you. See?"

"Oh, yes, I do! It WOULD be awkward, wouldn't it? And my mother would be so upset if I got thrown out of College – especially at this stage. She's denied herself a lot to send me here."

"That's what I mean! Besides which – it would finish me, too... Not that I'd worry much, I suppose."

"So what are you going to do?"

"Don't know yet! When I get faced with problems like this – or even problems quite unlike this – I usually drink a lot of beer."

"That's silly! It doesn't solve anything."

"Depends how you look at it. Beer has a knack of arranging things in a proper sequence of importance. It always brings the importance of beer to the forefront, for one thing; and the importance of sex, for another. And there isn't much I like more than beer-flavoured sex – two of the really natural things left in the world."

"The problem's still there, though, isn't it? THAT doesn't go away. Getting drunk only makes it SEEM un-important, doesn't it?"

"Well, if it seems unimportant, as far as I'm concerned, it IS unimportant. Or have I missed the point, somewhere?"

"What IS the point?"

"Well, at the moment – how nice you LOOK, for one thing. And how nice you ARE, for another. Two very important points."

"Glad you think so! That reminds me. You haven't noticed my belt."

She got up from the stool that she had found to sit on.

He gazed at the wide belt round her waist.

It had a large medallion, sewn in as a clasp, over her navel.

How on earth had he missed seeing it sooner?

Recent bastardy must have shaken him more than he had realized. He would have to get a grip on himself. He couldn't go round NOT noticing things, especially things like that, could he?

His survival depended on seeing and sensing what people were up to.

"It's got your name on," she said.

"Where?" he asked, in surprise.

Valerie undid the clasp, took off the belt, and pointed to his name on the concavity, inside the medallion.

"I had it engraved!"

He was profoundly touched.

"Why?" he asked, foolishly.

"Don't ask stupid questions."

"I'm good at asking them! It's one of the few activities I've had a lot of practice at, and do really well. So why shouldn't I indulge—?"

"—I made it!"

"Made it! That's marvellous! All this leather and wood and metal! Who did the metal bits for you?"

"I did! Upall showed me how to file the shapes, and polish them, and everything."

"So he can do something else, as well, can he? You ARE a talented lass, and no mistake. I've always wanted a mistress who was a first-class metal-worker and carpenter!"

She ignored this.

"Arnold?"

"Yes?"

"Do you really mean what you say?"

"Most of the time – no!... What have I said?"

"About the important things! The way I look, and so on."

"Those? Yes, I mean them! They seem to matter. Not only SEEM, but actually DO. A lot!... Why?"

"I've been thinking!... Why not let Sofia go ahead? Give her the evidence!"

"Now – be careful! Aren't you letting your tongue run away with you?"

"No, I'm not!" said Valerie, emphatically. "But sometimes I wish it would; I'd be a willing follower."

"What a little beauty you are, aren't you?"

"Am I?"

"I'll say!... I don't mind providing the evidence. In fact – I'll enjoy it! Grrr! That's the easy bit. The hard bit – will be admitting it. In public!"

"Yes!"

"Why don't we supply some now?" he asked, beginning to rise from his kitchen chair.

"Sit down! Not here! Among all this livestock?"

She shuddered.

"No! I want to see the rest of this place."

"You'll be sorry!"

She moved over to where he was sitting, fastening her belt round her waist, as she did so. Then, she bent over him and kissed him gently. He rested his forehead between her breasts.

"Val, I love the smell of you!"

Then, realizing the seriousness of what he was saying, added: "It's like one of Miss Clatworthy's oven-sticks!"

"Beast!... I love the smell of you, too!" she said.

Then, in retaliation: "Except for the beer, that is."

"I haven't got a smell! Only beer."

"You have. And it's nice."

At that moment she noticed a piece of paper on the table near his glass.

"What's that?" she asked.

He lifted his head from her sternum.

"Oh, that! Nothing much!"

He removed one hand from her waist, picked up the sheet and scruntled it into a ball.

"Why did you do that? Let me see it!"

She leaned across, took the ball from the table, smoothed it out and read it with a little smile on her face. Then, she looked up at Jonty, indulgently.

"Oh, so it's you, is it?" she crooned, in the manner of a fond mother to a child.

"Is what me?"

"Who pins up those rude notices all over the College? Everybody thinks it's students."

"That's what everybody's meant to think!"

"What will you do if Principal Polly Clatworthy finds out?"

"How?"

"I might tell her!" said Valerie, coyly.

"Short of inaugurating an Aunty Polly Finger-Print Day, that is the only way she'll ever find out."

Valerie giggled.

"I like this one."

"Which?"

"INSTANT NON-FATTENING EDUCATION SERVED HERE."

"Okay! We'll put that one up next."

"What's this other one for? It says JOIN THE SMOKER'S ABATEMENT SOCIETY."

"Oh, I dunno! Might come in handy, sometime. But it's in the draft stages. I'm still working on it."

Valerie looked around the kitchen in disgust, saying:

"This place needs a few notices of it's own, doesn't it?"

"Such as?"

"TIPPING RUBBISH IN THE KITCHEN NOT ALLOWED, she said, putting the capital letters into her voice.

Jonty laughed.

"Hey! You're coming on!"

"Pat Higgs has got a landlady who puts up notices all over the house. Pat says she's a real old cow! It's one of the ways she gives orders to her hubby. They haven't spoken to each other for seven years. He finds things pinned to the bathroom or lavatory door, or wherever, like: DINNER TONITE AT SEVEN. She can't spell for toffee!... others say things like SWITCH OFF LITES AT ALL TIMES."

Valerie wrote down the spellings for Jonty to see.

He was delighted!

She put this one up in Pat's room: PLEASE PUT CICKARET ENDS IN RESEPTIKLE PROVIDED. Pat's a non-smoker!"

"Well, she got PROVIDED right!"

"And this one in her bedroom: NO SMOCKING IN BED. THANK YOU VERY MUSH."

Jonty laughed again.

"I've always wanted to do some of that in bed."

"Smoking?"

"No! SMOCKING. Sounds rude."

"It isn't. It's a kind of stitch. Embroidery. I could show you some fancy smocking, if you like!" said Valerie innocently.

"In bed?" Jonty asked, leering exaggeratedly. "You know, I've never been to bed with you!"

"You have! Don't you—?"

"—I mean, literally. Why don't we remedy that at once?"

"Not now," said Valerie quickly. "Afterwards."

"After what?"

"After I've seen the mausoleum upstairs."

"Oh, that!... Well, you asked for it. Don't blame me if you go into shock!"

"I won't."

10

After Valerie had overcome the trepidation of her first encounter with 5 Griffield Road, she visited Jonty regularly there. If they wished to meet, it was the only place they could use; neither her rooms nor the College were safe places to be seen in, together.

In a week or so, she had overcome her aversion to the gothic sordidness of the building and its decrepit airs, its bizarre fittings and decor; and she had begun to enjoy the touches of panache provided by Mr Bennet's love of pageantry – such as the impeccable brightness of Leo.

She started to sleep overnight, usually on a Saturday, when she could give an excuse to her landlady that she was going to visit her mother.

On this Colchester Sunday morning, they had woken up early and made love and dozed off again. Now, she was lying awake, very still, listening to the singing of birds, with her head on Jonty's chest, seemingly asleep.

Jonty lay on his back. He had been awake for some time, and had begun to compose a letter to his mother in his head.

'Dear Mom,

'It's been a long spell since I last wrote to you. There didn't seem much to report, except the usual bastardy. This is different. I told you Dad had won a packet on the Pools, and I seem to have won a prize, too – a packet of real woman who goes night blind, so we have to keep the light on a lot of the time, but I enjoy committing adultery in the light and committing it as often as I can with her – the pleasures of which you never told me about for some reason. So does she. Her name is Valerie. But there's so much I haven't told you about her that I'd better let it come out a bit at a time, just as it wants to. She makes the stones of bastardy grind less harshly. And she knows how to handle me. Not many people know that, and no other woman has found out how to do it – except you, of course. You'd like her, I know. I wonder—.'

"—What are you thinking about?" asked Valerie suddenly, interrupting his silent composition, her head still resting on his chest.

"Oh, are you awake?" asked Jonty, startled. "This and that, this and that."

And added in his head: *'Can't write more just now. Back later.'*

"I've been awake for some time. Listening to your heart," she said. "Every so often it skips right up into my ear. Tuppety! Like that. It's funny!... Tell me what about."

In reply, he stroked her breasts, pausing to favour both of the small firm nipples at the tender middle of his palm for a moment, and then moved his hand slowly down to her stomach, letting it come to rest between her thighs.

"About this, mainly," he said.

She touched him in return with the tips of her fingers, watching herself do it.

"And I've been thinking about him. Will it always be this good for us?"

"I don't know. I hope so!... It keeps getting better. That's what's so incredible."

"Isn't it always like that?"

"No."

"What was it like with the others?... Once, you said you'd tell me. Will you?"

"Why?"

"Can't say! I just feel I want to know everything there is to know about you!"

"I understand the feeling! But it isn't possible, is it?... Anyway, women don't usually want to know about such things!" he added grumpily.

"How do you know what women want to know?" she said, pouting, and sitting up quickly, so that her breasts quivered.

Jonty laughed.

"Twaggin told me!" he said.

"Who's Twaggin?"

Briefly, Jonty told her something about Twaggin.

"Now, tell me about the others," she said decisively, settling her head back onto his shoulder.

He put an arm about her.

"You just won't be put off, will you?"

"No. I want to know the people who've mattered to you! It'll make me feel I belong to you, then. Tell me about Alexis... What was it like with Alex?"

He sighed.

"Oh! Alex. You might not like the way I tell it."

"I don't care how you tell it! I want to know. Tell me! I want to learn!"

"All right!" he said, resigned to her will.

Satisfied, she settled her head more deeply into his shoulder, lying half on her side, her small loosely clenched hand resting on his chest. She brought up a knee and rested it across his thighs, contentedly.

"Alex is a compulsive," he began. "Alex kept on wanting to get wedged, even just after you'd wedged her."

"Isn't that what they call nymphomania?"

"I suppose so!... But it wasn't just anybody. She had preferences. Maybe she just liked it more than most. I don't know... How can I describe it?... For her, the world was full of cucumbers and she wanted them all at once... now! – this minute! –and wanted them all the while – but, at the same time, it wasn't just any one of them that would do... Strange!... No, it was only certain ones. And they didn't have to be big and juicy! They could be – Oh, I dunno! Maybe she went by the colour? Or maybe she was looking for curly ones? I don't know!"

"Was it good with her?"

"It was good all right! She was fierce – a cucumber-swallower, a blood-drinker, a stoat! She turned me into a stoat. All furry whipping animal! But that was the trouble. That's how it stayed... I felt like some faceless piece of wild life... Go on! said Alex. She wanted you in. She wanted you to go on and on, until you couldn't move... She couldn't be bothered with the usual firkeydoodle. Not unless she did it herself!"

"What's firkeydoodle?"

"All the lead-up. What the sex manuals delicately term – foreplay. Not to be confused with backplay, lobs or forehand drives."

"Isn't that unnatural?"

"Well, well! A real male chauvinist!... No! I don't suppose so. Some women are like that – natural tennis players!"

"This firkeydoodle – what did she do?"

"My! What a clinical little bastard you are! Don't you want to know about Sofia?"

"All right. Tell me about Sofia."

"Why should I?"

"Don't you want to?"

"I suppose I don't mind... It was bloody good with Sofia. God, it was good!"

"Better than with me?"

"I thought you wanted to hear about it with Sofia?"

" I do."

"Well, stop being jealous!"

"I'm not! I just wanted to – Never mind! Continue with the lesson, Mr Godley, sir!"

"Sexually, she sent me frantic. And mentally, too. But in opposite directions."

"I don't send you frantic, do I?"

"Shall I stop interrupting you?"

"No, I'm listening!"

"Okay!… Sofia churned me up. But the strange thing was, she was never churned up. I got the impression that she regarded it as just another chore – like shopping – and when you ran out of sugar, you just popped out and bought some more."

"Didn't she like it?"

"Oh, she liked it all right!… Who doesn't?… But she made me feel like a stud bull hired out for routine servicing. And she happened to be a heifer that started me pawing the ground and whirling about on its haunches."

"First, stoats! Now, bulls and heifers! Aren't those metaphors a bit mixed up?"

"I daresay! But that's the way it comes. Take it or leave it!… Maybe you'd like me to give you exact vaginal dimensions? And refer to it by the catalogue numbers of the hundred and twenty eight positions?"

"How many?" asked Valerie, in astonishment.

"All right, hundred and twenty nine! I didn't think you knew that one."

"You are a fool, Arnold! I don't know any."

"Yes, you do!"

"Oh, well – those! That's not what I meant."

"I mean it! I mean it more each time."

"Arnold?"

"Yes?"

"Is it different with me?"

Jonty wriggled himself lower and kissed the nipple nearest to him, while his fingers moved between her thighs.

"Ooooh! That's so nice!" she said, wiggling her hips.

"Beautiful!... There's no doubt about it – you've got all the wherewithal... Mmm! And so neat. Unsensual. Designed for the job."

"That's not a nice thing to say! I want to be sensual."

"Well, YOU are, but IT isn't!"

"That doesn't make sense!"

"Yes, it does! Everything I say makes sense; most of what other people say makes non-sense. That's the way I define it... Therefore, it makes sense... I can't quite explain it. Your actual equipment ISN'T sensual. Not the way Sofia's was, or Alex's. But YOU are! You're so much more *foutable* than they were."

"It's because I want it!"

"No, I don't think so!" Jonty said, carefully. "Lots of women want it, and want it unbearably. I think it's more to do with – because you want it from ME."

"Oh, I do, I do!"

"Now?"

"No, not now. Let's talk some more afterwards. Talking makes it so much nicer."

"And talking before. And during. And all the time... That's another thing I like it with you for. You want me to talk to you... With Sofia it was always silent. A grinding silence!" he said, and laughed. "And mostly in the dark. She never wanted to talk."

"What about Alex?"

"She couldn't! Nearly unconscious with wanting it, she was. You were just something tromboning away. After her initial choice of musician, she didn't care much what you played. It was the sheer physical futtering she was after. Not that she'd stop you talking. Oh, no! She simply went deaf! But Sofia would tell you to shut up! Right in the middle, too. She said it was kinky to talk about it while you were doing it... You don't think it's kinky, do you?"

"No! I love you to talk to me while you do it. It tells me you know who I am. Do you know what I mean?... It's very very nice!... It's – oh, I don't know – human! Undoggy! Do you know what I mean?"

"I know exactly what you mean."

"Arnold?"

"Yes?"

"Why do you think those things were behind the bath?"

"What things – all those Victorian advertisements for corsets and shaving soap wrappers?"

"No! The others!"

"Oh, them!... Somebody dropped them there, I suppose."

"I know, idiot!... But why? Do you think they'd been used?"

"Of course!"

"But why there – behind the bath?"

"Guess!"

"I can't!"

"Maybe they did it in the bath and that was the nearest—"

"—You mean with water in!"

"What else?... Beer might be better, come to think of it."

"Can you do it in water?"

"Yes. Better in beer, though. Just think of all that froth round your—"

"—Arnold! Let's make love in the bath! In lovely warm water! Now!"

She jumped out of bed, searched naked for a moment, found Jonty's dressing gown, and put it on.

"You're an impulsive little devil, and no mistake... All that white and grey and mottled and black and cracked Italian marble! You said yourself it reminded you of a sarcophagus. You can hardly climb in and out of it!"

"That's what will make it exciting!"

"I'll do it on one condition."

"What's that?"

"We light that enormous bloody geyser and let it guddle and gurgle all through, to cover up your screams of ecstasy."

"Oh, you are a fool! I don't make a noise."

"You do! I'm thinking of getting a pair of ear-plugs."

"Liar!"

"Okay! You go up and light the geyser and run the water. I'll come up in a minute! When the coast is clear," he added, touching the sleeve of the dressing gown she had wrapped around her.

"All right!"

Valerie went out quickly and left Jonty still lying on his back in bed. He was watching a butterfly that had got into the room. It was fluttering round a cluster of bas-relief leaves in one corner modelled on the cornices of the ceiling that some enthusiastic earlier tenant without taste had attempted to paint realistically.

"You silly little bugger!" he said, sympathetically. "You'll get no change out or them!"

As he watched the flutterings of the butterfly on the ceiling, he began to muse on its dilemma.

'How do you explain the difference between the real and the artificial to an insect which doesn't already know?

'It was a pity you couldn't transmit knowledge like that directly through the genes, the way you could transmit a big nose or a little John Thomas, wasn't it?

'It seemed very much the same with people. If you tried, and they didn't already know the difference, you just couldn't get it across to them.

'Was it absolutely necessary that each generation make the same mistakes as its parents' and reach the point they had reached in much pain and strife, just when you were ready to pack it all up and lie down beside them for good?

'Why couldn't I know the Valerie-relationship was the one for me without going through the Alexis-and-Sofia experience first?

'And how can I tell her it is?'

Jonty sighed, and decided to resume his letter to his mother.

'Where did I get to?... Ah, yes! *"Back later."* That was it....

'Mom, I'm back now and I didn't mean what I said about adultery! That was being slick. It feels very different. It's in another league. There's nothing furtive about it, nothing prohibited, nothing – can't think of a better way to say it, and coming from me it must sound bloody odd – nothing sinful! That's the word! Do you know what I mean? We're not legally entitled, but that doesn't seem to count. With the others, it was sex AND love – or so I thought – two different things, but they went together. The sex seemed a way to reach the love. It felt as if there was a road through sex to love. AM I MAKING SENSE? But with Val, they feel like the same thing – as if the sex-part is only a way of expression for the love-part. In order to love her properly I must do the act of sex with her, but – and this sounds daft – the sex, for itself, doesn't seem to matter. In fact, it feels irrelevant, but still necessary. AM I MAKING SENSE? She doesn't churn me up. She doesn't suck all the juice out of me. I don't feel as if I'm driving for miles through a huge city at night, where I run out of fuel in some tumbledown area without a garage. That's how it felt with Sofia. Even worse with Alexis. I had no idea at all of the territory I was in. But Valerie fills up my tank with 110 octane by just being nearby. I feel as if my engine will go on forever, umpteen miles to the gallon, and after we've made love I've still got a lot of power left under the pedal. Mom, do you know what I'm talking about? If you do, explain it me, will you? Now, guide me home. I miss what you could teach me. But I remember what you did teach me. Every word, I think. And Valerie? How does she think of me? Am I her Valerie? Or shall I turn out to be one of her Alexises or Sofias, mistakes on the way? Why are there far more questions than answers? When I find answers, how shall I know they're the right ones? Mom, I've got to go now. She's waiting. Look after yourself. Miss you.

'Your loving son, Arnold.'

Jonty sighed again and got out of bed.

'Why the hell do I have to keep THINKING about things?'

Wasn't it enough for him that, when he was angry, she made him gentle; when morose, she made him smile; when aggressive, loving?

She could do all those things – by talking to him and by being herself! She would say: "Look at me, Arnold! Look at me... You're going away. Don't go away from me. Come back! I'm here. I want you with me, here. Come back to me, Arnold. Come back!"

She said it with such sadness and pleading and love that he returned from wherever it was he had been going and yielded himself willingly to her.

Then, it was all over.

What he had been feeling, he felt no longer; in its place was something so much more alive and responsive. It was all so much nicer than anything he had known before.

How did a scrap of a girl like her, a mere nineteen years old, a student being taught how to teach – how did she know how to do that – something women (and men) twice her age would have no idea about at all?

It was a bloody mystery!

Jonty suddenly remembered that Valerie was wearing his dressing-gown and stopped searching for it. He found an old raincoat instead and put that over his nakedness. As he was buttoning it up, the company of little doorbells began all over Bennet's Folly to tinkle their carillon of acknowledgment to the landlord's sense of pageantry and occasion.

"Bite him, Leo!" Jonty said, immediately.

But the ringing of bells went on; so Jonty concluded that Leo had continued to sleep.

"Lazy old bastard!" he muttered.

11

Jonty went through the passage by the staircase and into the hallway that had no pretensions. He opened the vestibule door, with its coloured mosaic of leaded-lights, and then the heavy front one.

Under his mackintosh, he felt decidedly chilly.

He was facing a plump woman in a damson-coloured felt-hat and a Royal-blue tweed suit. She held a sheaf of pamphlets in one hand and a torch in the other.

Jonty looked pointedly at the torch.

She began to smile sweetly at Jonty, until she noticed his thin bare legs sticking out below his raincoat. Her smile faded before it could flourish.

It must have been borne in on her that Jonty had nothing on underneath.

"Oh!" she said. "I'm very sorry to disturb you at this hour of the morning. Shall I—?"

"—That's all right! It's already nine o'clock and I was just going to have a shave... I'm sorry! I don't read *The Watchtower*," he said, staring at the pamphlets in her hand.

"Oh, these!" said the woman, looking down at them for a moment. "I'm not—"

"—Why have you got a torch?" interrupted Jonty.

"Ah, yes! Well, I won't keep you a minute, Mr – er – Mr—. May I ask if you are the householder?"

"Yes."

"Good! Well, you see I'm canvassing—"

"—On a Sunday morning!"—

"—for the local elections. And I was wondering if—"

"—What party?"

"Oh, the Labour Party, of course! And—"

"—Sorry! We're all Christians, here," said Jonty, retreating into the vestibule. "Apart from those of us who are nudists, that is," he added, through the closing door.

As he was about to close the vestibule firmly up, he heard a scuffling sound from outside. The canvasser was stuffing papers under the door.

His immediate impulse was to stuff something else, bigger and stiffer, back to her; but he had nothing handy. There was not even a forgotten newspaper knocking about. He did the next best thing: he stepped forward and opened the door quickly.

The woman was still stooping and nearly fell inwards.

"Would you like to come upstairs and scrub my back?" asked Jonty, blandly. "I've decided to have my monthly bath while you're here."

Still crouching, her face expressed amazement.

"Or maybe you'd prefer to scrub it here?" he asked.

When she didn't move, he began to undo the top buttons of his mackintosh.

"I could fetch a bowl."

Then, plump as she was, the woman stood up with alacrity. Her expression became aggressive: it was clearly not the first time she had had to deal with propositions of this kind.

"You are disgusting, and I shall report you to the—"

"—Well, stop stuffing litter under my door! Or I'll be doing some reporting myself."

She said no more. She turned and, despite her size, scuttled off down the path, her rump and torch wagging rhythmically.

"Bloody politics!" he said, in disgust, quite loud enough for her to hear. She continued on her way.

Jonty went up the marble staircase two at a time and arrived in the bathroom to find the antiquated geyser all fired-up with enthusiasm, raring to go. It was making deep abdominal gurglings and guddling away distractedly in its entrails. The sarcophagus was half-full, and Valerie was stretched out in it, one foot held under the trickle of warm water that had been persuaded to reach the faucets.

"I love warm water," she said, sinking a little further into it.

"I've just made up my mind about something," said Jonty.

"What?"

"They're super-doopers, not doopers."

He leaned over the white marble ledge to better appreciate the way the water buoyed up her breasts, and to cup his hands under them.

"What comes before doopers?" asked Valerie.

"Nibbinses and nubbinses."

"Which are which?"

"Nibbins are what you'd call – a pair of gnat bites."

"Like Miss Crawford's?"

"I'm not sure. I'm inclined to think she may actually have hollows."

"Women don't have hollows there. Don't be silly!"

"All right, I won't!... How's this for being sensible?"

He hopped over the high marble side of the bath, across its wide marble ledge, and into the water, and lay full-length on top of her, his lips closing on her nipple.

"Mminm! Lovely!" she sighed. "But why didn't you take your mack off, first?"

"Oh, yes! I forgot!" he said, sitting up and removing it.

"It's all sopping wet, now!" she said. "Oh, Arnold, look!"

She pointed at his chest.

"What?" he asked, looking down.

"You've gone all spotty!"

"Oh, Christ! Has that started again?"

"Stand up!" she said. "Have you got it all over?"

"Oh, Yasus!" he moaned, standing up, naked. "Now she wants to issue me with a medical Certificate of Health... It must be your effect on me. You make me break out in a rash. Shall I turn round? Do you want to inspect the rear premises, as well?"

"No! Be serious. What is it?"

"I don't know!"

"How long have you had it?"

"It came recently. Warm water seems to start it off. These little red spots come up. Sometimes it happens without a bath. If you scratch one, it gets bigger. Here – do you want to try?"

"Yes!"

She scratched one on his thigh.

"So they do!" she said. "Do they go away again?"

"Now look what you've done to me, scratching there!"

"I am looking!... Do they go away?"

"Off and on! Am I repulsive?"

"Don't be silly! It doesn't make any difference."

"I'm glad! Because look what you did."

"I know! I have looked. Is it time? Is the water too deep? Do you think we shall drown?"

"Who cares?"

"I don't!... Try now," she said. "I want to try now!"

Jonty sank into the water and took her in his arms, easing himself into her body. She responded at once.

"Oh, God! I never want it with anyone but you, Arnold. I don't! I don't!"

"That's my girl," said Jonty. "That's my lovely girl!"

12

A week later, Jonty was still worrying about the sudden re-appearance of his spots.

He felt immensely grateful to Valerie that she had in no way let them bother her. They certainly did not diminish her physical passion for him and she seemed to love him just the same.

This was a source of surprise to Jonty; he wondered how he would have reacted if he'd found out at a particularly intimate moment in the bath that his lady-love rivalled a spotted dog – in numerical terms, that is, if not in colouration, or other respects.

Would he have been so unaffected?

He didn't know. It made him admire Valerie even more than he had before.

The upshot of his disquietude was an appointment he had made secretly with a skin specialist at the Colchester Hospital.

So much the better if he could manage to get rid of the blemishes! If not, he would at least know what kind of terrible affliction had come upon him.

He had even wondered whether it was something sent to him from On High because of his persistent adulteries with Valerie and his betrayal of the trust in *loco parentis* that Aunty Polly Clatworthy had lovingly laid upon him when he took the job.

But he had dismissed these suspicions as signs of hysteria and decided rationally instead to consult professional opinion.

Thus, he had gone through all the boring details of registration as an out-patient, and was now facing Dr Muller in a room that reeked of anti-septic and was full of all the usual hospital paraphernalia, waiting – stripped to the waist, after undergoing his preliminary examination – for the great man's verdict.

Dr Muller's bespectacled blue eyes and fleshy face were beaming: a pale beacon of joy that irradiated even the darkest corners of his Examination Trolley.

"This is absolutely magnificent, Mr Godley!"

Without animation, Jonty scrutinized the enchanted features of the specialist.

'Well, why doesn't it bloody FEEL magnificent?' he thought. 'Next week, Starring Spotty Arnold Jonty in – The Magnificent Hordes. Ta-Ra! With a Cast of Thousands.'

"See!" said the doctor, rapturously. "When I scratch them, they stand up and go red."

'Supposing I did that to you? Wouldn't you stand up and go that?'

The doctor peered again at Jonty's chest.

The expression of rapturous joy remained on his face. His index finger was poised and crooked over another of Jonty's spots, ready to scratch it vigorously with his fingernail.

He was a young man, full of energy.

"There's no doubt at all, Mr Godley. It goes along with this related skin condition of yours. Turn over, please! There! I can write on you. Sit up! Look in that mirror!.. Dermographia!... See the long cursive strokes coming up in red? It's quite remarkable!... A very rare disease. Five per cent of the population at the most... You're a patient in a thousand Mr Godley. Literally!... You can stand up, now, Mr Godley. Thank you!"

Jonty sat up and let his legs dangle over the side of the Examination Trolley, as if he had forgotten how to use them.

Dr Muller was writing something onto a large card on his desk. Suddenly, he turned and made straight for Jonty.

"Please stand up for a moment, Mr Godley."

'Yaysus! What's he going to write on me, now?'

The doctor peered at Jonty's neck, just below the ear.

'Is he going to scratch on in upper case: IF YOU CAN PEE THIS HIGH JOIN THE FIRE BRIGADE?'

Dr Muller's fingers were scraping away, conscientiously.

"Thanks! That's fine!" he said, at last.

"Look, doctor," said Jonty, who could bear no more scouring, "I know I'm a unique specimen, but that doesn't make up for having *graffiti* written all over me, does it?"

The doctor straightened up and smiled.

"Would you mind, Mr Godley? Just stay like that. I'd like to fetch my camera."

'What now – a feature movie?'

Dr Muller waited for Jonty's reply.

Jonty said nothing.

When Jonty remained silent, the doctor asked again:

"Would you mind very much if I took a photograph of you?"

Jonty, still involved with his suspicions, asked: "Is it in Technicolor?"

"What?... Oh! Oh, I see – well, it's a colour slide, if that's what you mean. I can't let an opportunity like this slip away. It's exactly what I need to illustrate a set of lectures I'm giving at the University... Do you mind being immortalized as a Case History, Mr Godley?"

"You're sure you're not bringing it out on the front page of *The News of the World*?"

Dr Muller laughed heartily.

"Not at all, Mr Godley. A paragraph in *The Colchester Gazette* at the most, I promise... I shan't be a moment!"

Dr Muller turned and almost skipped out of the room in his eagerness to fetch his camera.

Well, there it was!

Not a punishment of the Almighty's, after all. But a disease for the select few! An elitist affliction called *Urticaria Pigmentosa.*

Perhaps he should feel proud of it?

He might even be able to use it against The Pettigrew in some subtle way, for, almost certainly, she would not have heard of it.

But that wasn't all!

It seems it went along with another condition, just as unusual, that allowed doctors to write rude slogans on people's skins!

Furthermore, if he made a point of sitting on cane-bottomed chairs, he could carry the pattern around with him for at least fifteen minutes after he had got up.

Could he turn it into a party trick?

He wondered if he could even make money out of it. How many performances a day could he stand? Troubles and blessings never came singly, did they?

The doctor returned with his Pentax.

"Dr Muller," said Jonty, "what's the best cure for this condition?"

The doctor smiled broadly.

"Oh, it's incurable!" he said, cheerfully. "It comes of its own accord and goes away when it feels like it. Just like warts! Various treatments have been tried, but none of them works. We know next to nothing about the affliction. I COULD give you anti-histamines, I suppose."

Jonty's spirits rose.

"But they won't be a bit of use," added Dr Muller, happily.

He flourished his camera at him.

"Stand facing the wall, please! That's right, Mr Godley. Hands on hips. Hollow the chest. Hold your breath. That's lovely!"

There was a flash and the doctor asked Jonty to turn round.

"Now the front. Stay! That's lovely."

The camera flashed again.

"Beautiful! Well, that's about all we can do, Mr Godley."

"Do I have to keep off the beer, doctor? Or something just as terrible?"

"No! Not at all. Beer might help. Who knows?... We think it's a sign of stress of some kind. Or even nervous exhaustion. Perhaps, even physical exhaustion... You can put your shirt on again, Mr Godley," said the doctor, writing again on his file-card. "You're not worrying about anything, are you?" he asked, casually.

Jonty shut his eyes, drew a large breath and prepared himself to repulse any such idea; but before he could do so, the doctor's question had had its effect.

The forces of bastardy formed up in their platoons before his eyes; they marched steadily before him, their tackety boots thunderous on the Parade Ground.

Dummock was at their head, swinging his mace; Treblitt, the Big Drum; The Pettigrew and Big Rev, on brass; then surprisingly, Crehan, fluting sturdily; and, behind him, slightly less audible, Sir Leslie and Spouse; and they were all followed by the faceless and silent legion, squads of horrible hypnagogic O'Grady's moving purposefully through the dawn smog.

"Are you all right, Mr Godley?" asked the doctor.

Jonty began to open his eyes just as Sar'nt Major Polly Clatworthy was giving orders to fix bayonets

Hurriedly, he focussed on the doctor:

"Me! Worried? God, no!... Except for these spots, I don't have a care in the world, doc!"

"That's just splendid, Mr Godley, just splendid! Don't think about them! If you take my advice, you'll forget that they are there!"

'Easier said than done, doc!'

"Come and see me again if there's anything fresh happening, won't you?"

"You mean if they start barking, or growing little leaves, or something?"

"Ha, ha! There's no fear of that, Mr Godley. They can't harm you. Just treat them like friends. Well – goodbye and good luck, Mr Godley."

"Goodbye, doctor, and thanks!"

They shook hands and Dr Muller hit the button of a little silver bell on his desk to call in the next patient.

Jonty turned mournfully away and left.

It was true, he had none on his face and they didn't itch. Nobody but Valerie would know that they were there.

However, HE knew they were there, didn't he?

…Treat them like friends, indeed!

…Maybe it was good advice, though – because – how did you treat friends? Answer: you bought them noggins. Didn't you?

…And that was precisely what he was going to do; he and all his friends could get stotius together. He looked at the clock in the Entrance Hall of the hospital. They were open. He had fully two hours before the monthly Staff Meeting at two p.m.

Well, maybe not stottin' – but certainly merry!

Two hours later, having made his way back carefully to St Anne's, the suspicion had been growing that he had backed a dark horse each way and, although it was well-placed, he was now watching the favourite come up fast on the outside.

He was sucking vigorously at a well-known circular mint, hoping that the aroma of Greene & King's best bitter – which mixed uneasily with the odours of cosmetic lotions, perfumes and female deodorants that swirled about him – might escape through the hole in its middle; meanwhile, he looked round at his odoriferous colleagues squeezed into the long tables that had been placed end-to-end in the Music Room for the meeting.

Primarily, they seemed to be discussing their favoured topics: hairdresser's appointments, eye-level grillers, self-timing ovens, and – when, how and why – who had done what to whom; except Doris Crawford, that is, who was reading a magazine for cat owners.

One of the Persians off-colour, was it?

Most of the men doodled silently and disconsolately on the little white pads that had been placed on the tables in front of each place.

Big Rev was fingering his fleshy nose, thoughtfully. Checkmate?

They all waited. Aunty-General Clatworthy – he had re-promoted her in his mind since the doctor's question – was late. This was very unusual: something important must have delayed her; at least, something consequential to her.

At the last Staff Meeting, Jonty had been requested to re-draft the English Syllabus, ready for the next edition of the College Calendar.

The Aunty-General wished the prescribed texts to be closer to the surmised interests of the type of student she wished to produce.

Put more clearly, she had decided that the Syllabus should basically be an Anthology of excerpts that had to do with Cooking, Clothes and Deportment Through the Ages.

Of course, she didn't call it that openly: that was Jonty's expression.

Anything that showed the relationships of the sexes in a raw and uncooked condition was to be censored out.

But it was all right to include any bits he found that had been properly washed, had the eyes removed, half-baked, and served up with a discreet sauce.

However, the longer he had searched, the more difficult it had become; and he was wondering, now, how he was going to persuade the Principal that English writers did not see man-woman relationships in culinary terms, even though, on occasions, they might use gustatory and domestic images. They would persist in seeing the relationship between the sexes, sexually.

In Clatworthy language, they ate uncooked food with their fingers and then wiped them on their rumps.

It simply wasn't good enough, was it?

One expected better of the English Tradition!

Jonty had begun historically, writing out the Big Names in more or less chronological order; he had then intended to follow them with the chosen work...

So far, he had crossed out the names of Chaucer, Shakespeare, Jonson, Ford, Webster, Congreve, Sheridan, Fielding, Smollett, Richardson, Dryden, Lawrence and Dickens: all were too sexy for the General.

He seemed to be left with Swift, Pope, Scott, Jane Austen, Thackeray, Meredith, George Eliot, Barbara Cartland and Godfrey Winn.

Swift?

...Wasn't he suspect?... True, he WAS a Tory!... But what would General Clatworthy think of a writer who had let his hero piss all over a town to save it from devastation by fire?

Even if they were Lilliputians? And even if he was Dean of St Paul's?

'A thing like that isn't hygienic, is it, Mr Godley?

'And what about all the food in that town? I think you are aware of the stress we place on the necessity for clean food in our Housecraft Courses, Mr Godley? I'm afraid—'

Jonty sighed and crossed out the name of Jonathan Swift.

Owning a surplice of the Anglican Church, and being a master of the English Tongue, were clearly no guarantees of respectability in the eyes of Respectability.

But Jonty, having been on intimate terms with the Reverend F.E. Newey for a number of years, should have seen that; and should have known that the possession of several of them was no guarantee of anything, least of all, cleanliness. (Since arriving at St Anne's, Jonty had learned that godliness came after Cleanliness in the sequence of Christian virtues)... He went back to his list... Jane Austen?...Well, she was impeccable, at any rate.

'George Eliot. Oh, a lovely writer, Mr Godley!... Barbara Cartland. Very sound, Mr Godley! There is no other writer in the English Language who sees the virtues of balanced meals for husbands better than she does... And we COULD put Dickens back on the list, couldn't we, Mr Godley? He was so fond of Christmas!... I'm glad you agree with me... Godfrey Winn? Mmm! Don't you think he's a wee bit suggestive, at times?... No!... Well, all right! We'll compromise on Godfrey Winn, shall we?'

That left him six or seven unassailable classics of the English tongue: Jane Austen, Scott, Thackeray, Meredith, George Eliot, Dickens, Barbara Cartland and Godfrey Winn.

Pope, as a Roman Catholic, was doubtful, of course.

He could, he supposed, have added Aunty Wordsworth, Robert Louis Stevenson and – Pope Eliot – at a pinch.

But what the hell, Archie, what the hell?

They had more there than they would ever be able to read.

At the year's end, he would probably receive a plethora of theses on Mrs Cartland, a few on Mr Winn, maybe one or two on Miss Austen, and none at all on anybody else.

With luck, he wouldn't even need to re-read the other authors – or even to read a couple of them for the first time. Feeling he had discharged his duties as well as he could under the circumstances, Jonty sighed with relief, and put down his pencil.

At that point in his cogitations, the door of the Music Room opened and Aunty-General Polly Clatworthy limped in, not a single medal in evidence. She seemed to be finding trouble in putting the ball of one foot to the ground.

What was it? Bumblefoot?

And for some reason, she was holding her head on one side, too.

Newcastle disease? The bane of old hens.

Or had the General been assaulted on one of her weekly forays into the local pubs on Saturday night, distributing *The Watchtower* and continuing the good work of General Booth? Helped by her secretary, Miss Marchbanks (who was something big in the Girl Guides), she made her way across the Music Room to her seat at the head of the tables.

But her secretary would have been big out of the Guides, as well: she made the Principal look slim; she sat beside her Chief, her pencil poised, smiling about her, grandly.

After a rather grumpy "Good afternoon", the Principal explained that she had had a fall in a corridor of the College, sprained her ankle and twisted her back.

A number of the women "Oh'd" and "Ah'd" sympathetically, some whispered together, a few showed no reaction; the men looked vaguely concerned, and Big Rev murmured to himself.

She interrupted the chorus of concern and no-concern by saying loudly, as she leaned back in her chair:

"We've got to have a war on shoes, I think."

This pronouncement effected complete silence.

"A lot of footwear is unsuitable for walking around College," the Principal went on.

One or two of the more timid souls looked furtively downwards.

"And we have a very great responsibility to help students to dress tastefully and – seemlily."

The Principal felt uncomfortable with her last adverb and her eyes flickered for a moment in Jonty's direction, as if seeking some reassurance about its correctness.

Keeping his eyes fixed on a spot on the wall about four feet above Upall's long Yorkshire head, he refused to give any sign.

Slightly ruffled, the Principal proceeded to explain that it was the unsuitable footwear of a careless student that had caused her accident.

It appeared that the girl – the Principal ostentatiously forbore naming her – had been startled by the sudden appearance of the Principal in the corridor, had got up from where she had been indecorously sitting, tripped over the big clumsy heels of the shoes she was wearing, fell against the Principal, and down had come the Clatworthy tons with a resounding thump.

"Therefore –," continued Miss Clatworthy.

Jonty noted with interest the ominous touch of purple around the General's dewlaps, sensing that this was one round the more sophisticated women of the staff and the fashion Houses would NOT win. When the Principal eventually made her proposal, there was instant and general assent to the wisdom of it from the majority of the staff.

Jonty let his eyes descend slowly to Upall's face – who acknowledged him by trying to make his pupils contract and peer upwards into his cerebral lobes, failed, gave up, left his eyebrows suspended high over his sockets, rolled his eyes until only the whites showed, let his jaw drop, and gradually came back to normal.

It was one of the battery of visual protests he had devised to mourn the passing, in the course of the academic year, of a student sport or vice dubbed undesirable by the General.

Afterwards, Upall said he thought he had under-played it.

Jonty watched the owl-eyes of The Pettigrew flitting from face to face.

Didn't she ever tire of hunting for rodents?

After this bombshell of an introduction, the Principal formally opened the meeting, and the first item on the Agenda came up in due course for discussion: College Discipline.

'Ah, well, we all know what that is, don't we? We see enough of it.'

Miss Clatworthy began in her best contralto tones, the ones she used in the Salvation Army Choir, to inveigh: "I imagine you all know what this is about."

Jonty wondered if she might not convey her meaning better and more effectively, if she stopped wagging her arms about *aleggiarendo* like that.

It distracted people.

Was she getting ready for a Brigade Concert? Were conductor-contraltos uncommon in the musical world?

"The culprit must be ferreted out and punished. It's just got to stop! Immediate expulsion!... I suppose you've all seen the new one that appeared outside the Assembly Hall only yesterday?... What puzzles me is – they all seem to be written on College art-paper!..."

Her next question was intoned *vivace*:

"Have you got anything to say about this, Mr Upall?"

Upall started guiltily, but recovered himself at once.

Jonty had the strong intuition that Upall had been working out, in full Panavision, all the steps in his next seduction; and Jonty knew for a fact that Upall had his eye on a nice little ginger pussy in his Second Year Art Group.

Lucky girl!

However, he replied *delicatezza*, in some of his characteristic 'quickthink, sell-anything' *recitativo*:

"The only conclusion I can draw, Miss Clatworthy, is that somebody has got hold of a duplicate key. Of course," (now *giocoso*) "it's not impossible that a key has been specially made. After all, we do have a course in metal-work in the College, don't we?"

He ended *rallentando*, looked up and smiled happily at the rows of faces watching him, confident in the knowledge that he had sold them a good tune.

His ploy worked.

They began discussing his suggestions *con anima*. Iconoclast that he was, Upall saw, nevertheless, the percentage for himself in having a good stock of ready-made tunes and off-the-peg widgets for all occasions, which now, together with his *agilmente* North Country gab, energy and selling technique – employed *con forza* – had got them parading around nicely, practising on the brass and windy opinions he had lust sold them: too big in the mouthpiece, too narrow in the chanter, too tight in the slide, sticky-valved, off-key, too short in the tube, too dry in the reed; but all were perfectly happy with their bargains.

No doubt about it, Upall was a damn' good salesman!

They, for the most part, were tone-deaf and parade-conscious, and Upall exploited them shamelessly in his quest for self-advancement.

It was quite a performance!

Jonty breathed out joyfully, slowly: he found no difficulty in acknowledging a master.

A compliment was in order! He tore a sheet from his pad and scribbled a pithy comment on it.

Then, he passed it along the table.

Note-passing was a common practice during the solos from the Chair. Nobody would mind.

The note got stuck at Big Rev's.

He seemed to be *doloroso* under another of his toupees, changed since yesterday.

Building a wig wardrobe, was he?

His grand head rested on his enormous hand, a considerable thumb and first finger making a deep Vee through which his fleshy nose extruded.

Was he thinking of trying to conduct, too, with THAT?

Or working on a new opening chess gambit?

The Pettigrew leaned over and nudged him awake with a start.

His huge head nodded, hiding his nose for a moment: now you see it, now you don't!

She pointed to the folded square of white paper in front of him.

He became attentive, looked momentarily bewildered at The Pettigrew, then spotted the note and picked it up... Sleight of nose, be damned!

Attentomente, Big Rev began to open out the square of paper and smooth it down on the table in front of him.

Jonty groaned and began to curse him silently.

'Great unmentionable balls of unmentionable foulness!

'What does the silly big unprintable whatsit want to go and do that for? We know he can't read music. Let him stick to his comb-and-paper!... May his fingers turn into toes and develop bunions on all the joints!'

A red flush started to move up, *appassionato*, from the rim of his dog-collar. God knows where it had started from!

Jonty covered his face before it could reach Big Rev's toupee and groaned silently.

Big Rev sat as still as a stone, staring at Jonty's note.

It so happened that General Clatworthy had, at that moment, reached the point of reading out *molto forte* in her clear parade-ground contralto:

"IDEAS ACCEPTABLE ONLY IF WEARING TWENTY SIX INCH BOTTOMS AND THICK TURN-UPS OR HEAVY TWEED SKIRTS. COLOURED TIGHTS FORBIDDEN.

"And that one," General Clatworthy vocalized, "found its way into the Main Entrance Hall of the College – for all our official visitors to see!"

Jonty began to feel that the enemy forces were gathering against him.

He fancied he could feel the pressure of the General's central pulmonic air-stream roaring into his eardrums. Its poundage per square inch was high. It expressed *agitato*.

He was surrounded by a massed chorus of tuttings. He was being pressed into a smaller and smaller space by the weight of them.

He felt unreal: he belonged in a story by Edgar Alan Poe, not here in this Military Band of Purity.

He wailed inwardly.

'Oh, why, oh why, did I have to put that notice up in the Main Entrance Hall and why do I keep on being a bloody fool? Furthermore, why such a bloody fool? And why did I have to go and write that stupid message to George Upall JUST BLOODY NOW?'

Big Reverend's intimidating head was swinging round, *adagio*, in Jonty's general direction, roseate and outraged.

Eventually, he focussed on Jonty and stared at him, unwinkingly.

Completely still, slightly hunched, with his big pale nose and his vast pink face and his toupee partly awry, Big Rev looked more than ever like the top of the Company's Giant Mascot, arrested half-way through his make-up before the Big Parade, having come, at last, face-to-face with Pure Evil.

Under his stare, Jonty began to quail.

13

Big Rev, as if going through some ceremony of Papal or Episcopal Purification, pressed, screwed and scruntled the paper of Jonty's note, *con moltissimo deliberato*, into a tight little ball. It was as tight as his powerful hands could make it.

Then, still with his eyes unlovingly on Jonty, he dropped it deliberately into the breast pocket of his worsted clerical jacket.

Even more threateningly, he turned away and, in slow motion, fixed his eyes on General Clatworthy at the head of the twin row of tables.

Jonty's heart sank.

What was he going to do, now? How could the General fail to notice the chameleon slowness of Big Rev's movements? Was he going to stand up, just as menacingly, draw himself with unhurried premeditation to his full six feet four, and sing an off-key solo on an all-too-familiar theme?

Jonty fancied he could feel his urticaria being urged into profuse and more luscious spot-making under his vest and shirt.

If Big Rev had not been immediately blinded by the superficial but powerful obscenity of the note, its implications must have been as clear as daylight to him: wasn't the General still inveighing against the Phantom Scribbler?

Big Rev's shoulders seemed to be rising very, very slowly under the yeast of his outrage.

Was he changing his mind, and was he now going to perform an oratorio of warning, in his *basso profondo*, about the suspected identity of the culprit; or a requiem for his death?

Should Jonty try decoy manoeuvres?

What about faking an epileptic fit – like the one he had witnessed in Kingmaker's lecture? Wouldn't that upset the Big Rev's performance a bit?

Or, alternatively, what about a long, loud and beautifully controlled fart, ended on a dying fall?

Wouldn't that provide a more appropriate finale to things? Who knows, he might even get asked for an encore!

But Big Rev, *tacet*, remained in his seat and, with his shoulders subsiding gently, the moment of danger passed. He lapsed into his characteristic chess-playing droop.

Jonty breathed a heavy sigh of relief and offered up a silent prayer to the Muse of Comedy that Big Rev's cymbal-shaped ears would, as of yore, continue to stand out at right angles to his head; that they would remain the virile percussion instruments they obviously were; that the salt applied to icy Winter roads would not splash up and rust the rivets, causing them to fall off in a traffic jam; and that he'd emerge victorious from most of his forthcoming chess contests.

He couldn't pray fairer than that, could he?

Eventually, with nothing resolved on the issue of the Phantom Scribbler, the Principal went on to discuss the next point on the Agenda: Assessment of Final Teaching Practice.

As usual with such topics, it promised to become a tedious exercise of fingering through an *arpeggio* of alternately flat notes of genteel outrage at student performances and, as they tried to be fair, the *sharp* ones of enlightenment.

After all, they were aware of what was at stake for students passing out to their chosen profession, weren't they?

Weren't they?

Bedimmed temporarily by the thick haze of his apprehensions, Jonty found he'd switched on again halfway through a *cantata da chiesa* on Miss Pike.

Had he not caught the hushed phrase of 'Mau-Mau' somewhere?

There was some kind of a solo going on, with passages of chorus work thrown in from time to time. Those against Miss Pike sang the loudest refrains.

One of the soloists in favour of the student under discussion was Doris Crawford, who was, at that very moment, trying to catch the conductor's eye, so that she could come in a few bars early.

But, alas, Ursula Pettigrew was in full spate.

Her *libretto* had something to do with Miss Pike's ancestors, who, she claimed, were Welsh; which, in turn, had some bearing on a lesson she had given on, surprisingly enough, the General Post Office. The Pettigrew, as visiting tutor, had been intrigued by a sentence written up by Miss Pike on the blackboard, in Welsh: it had said NAILV AN, as plain as plain. Ursula trilled this out loudly and clearly, while sitting up very straight on her steatopygian behind, as if looking over a music stand.

General Clatworthy glanced across at Mr Morgan, the College Welshman (who had been born in Blackpool) to invite him to translate. But Mr Morgan was baffled.

The Principal's eyes glinted with amusement; her chins wobbled, precariously. No wonder: Mr Morgan didn't know a word of Welsh. Everything about him was – except his surname and his liking for harp music – as English as an airedale.

…Could it be, by some far-flung coincidence, that Miss Pike was a founder member of the Welsh Nationalist Party, as well as of Mau-Mau?

The idea intrigued Jonty enormously; he immediately began to wonder what elements the parties could possibly have in common.

However, his speculations had to be discarded, as he simply had to listen to the lament The Pettigrew was in the middle of, at the moment.

"AND, Miss Clatworthy," called Ursula in her best *pizzicato*, "do you know what it turned out to be?"

The General waggled her dewlaps. The owl-eyes of The Pettigrew opened wider. She drew in her breath.

"It was Miss Pike's spelling of MAIL VAN," vibrato.

A lot of people laughed. The Pettigrew let her breath out through her nostrils in a snort of disgust.

"No, it wasn't!" said a loud jerky voice.

All eyes turned to look at Doris Crawford. Ignoring the score, was she, and doing it through a vamp-horn?

Delighted with the effect she had had, she gave a little gurgle, momentarily trying again to be one of those hot New Zealand geysers. Her loud-hailing tones rang out once more:

"How do you know this, Miss Crawford?" asked the General, coming in right on key.

"She's in my Personal Supervision Group. I read it in her School Practice Record. She noted it in her criticism of the lesson. It was to impress the children with the proper way to spell 'mail van'."

"Isn't that very odd, Miss Crawford, putting up something that is wrong, in order to show the children how to spell it correctly?"

"I've seen worse things in a classroom," mumbled Doris *dolcissima*.

Into the moment of silence that followed her reply, there came a crash like a bungled gear-change on a six-ton truck: Big Rev was clearing his throat. Everyone looked at him and waited politely.

Eventually, the General asked: "Yes, Reverend Heffler? I believe you wish to add to this?"

'Add to what?' thought Jonty. 'Furthermore, add what to what? Has he decided to renege on that oratorio decision? Because, if he has, I'll—'

"—Thank you, Miss Clatworthy!" he said, in his Paul Robeson voice. "I have been in a position to observe that, during the entire period of her Teaching Practice, the student in question has made a habit of going out at least twice a week with her – I hardly like to sound deprecating – her 'boy friend', usually to the detriment of her lesson preparations."

'Miss Pike, Miss Pike, cuddly as a rake! Good for her!'

Silenzio!

'That's funny! I don't remember the score indicating several bars rest, here.'

Their mouths were falling open. Jonty could hear them ill-thinking:

A boyfriend! Miss Pike! One of our maturest students? Nearing forty? Every line telling its story!… Unsavoury habits?… No! Are you quite, quite sure, Reverend, that you haven't—'

'Permissive behaviour' was his favourite topic: Big Rev was quite unaware of the sensation he had caused. His ears hadn't even trembled.

Once, Upall had told Jonty scathingly, Big Rev had put forward a motion, in the era of the miniskirt, stipulating that all tights and stockings worn in College be at least 60 denier lyle: this, he felt, would help combat the excesses of the current fashion. "But, really," said Upall, "to combat the general direction of his own thinking. Luckily, he lost that one. That's why he took to chess – a refuge from his own lust!"

The General was intervening again.

"Are you certain, Reverend, that we are talking about the same student? I find it rather unlikely – we all do, fear—"

Many heads nodded vigorously in agreement.

"Oh, quite certain, Miss Clatworthy! We ARE discussing Miss Prike, are we not?"

Miss Clatworthy sighed. She shook her head. Her dewlaps wobbled.

"No, Reverend Heffler," she said patiently. "I'm afraid we are not. This is a Miss Pike... Miss PRIKE is quite a different student, the kind of person you were—! A natural enough mistake, of course!"

"Oh! I'm most dreadfully sorry! I was quite sure we—"

"—That's quite all right, Reverend Heffler. We'll continue with—" She looked about her, waiting for further contributions from the floor. "—the discussion," she finished off.

'Let the silly bastard,' thought Jonty, 'go back to riffling through his pack of 30, 60 and 95 denier prejudices, and working out unusable chess gambits.'

Everybody knew that the Reverend Heffler didn't believe in self-indulgence; only in self-self-indulgence.

George Upall swore that, some time ago, Big Rev had asked Miss Lambert, the head of the Needlework Department, to embroider his pillows in coloured silks with the words: THOU SHALT NOT; and had asked Upall himself to print THE PRICE OF SIN IS EVERLASTING FIRE in 8 point Baskerville type on his pyjamas. Upall had refused, he said, 'on eschatological grounds. Besides, he had pinched the idea from Dylan Thomas and with a pyjama jacket that size, and a slogan that long, it would have absorbed too much ink.'

Jonty believed him. General Clatworthy startled Jonty by directing a remark at him.

"I believe you have relevant information for us, Mr Godley?"

"Oh! Have I?"

"Do you remember telling me about Hodder & Stoughton some time ago?" she asked, pronouncing the names as if they referred to well-known exponents of titanic acts of sexual perversion.

Jonty hadn't got the faintest recollection of having used either name in a pure or impure context, still less in open combat with the General, or of ever having enunciated them anywhere in his life. Then he remembered.

"Oh, I believe you mean J.M. Dent & Sons!"

"Do I?" replied Miss Clatworthy, blankly.

By the time the confusion was sorted out, the whole point of the anecdote – namely, to depress still further the depressing and depressed reputation of Miss Pike – had been mercifully ruined.

Jonty was glad, for her sake. Pike might be a funny kind of name for a forty-year-old trainee in a company of Houseguards but, by Gad! she has as much right in the Regiment as that timpani-bottomed Pettigrew, sir!

Jonty managed to doze fitfully through the names from P to V in the alphabet.

When he came to, he amused himself by trying to work out some correlation between the various degrees of bastardy he saw about him and the distances that ears stood away from heads. He felt he was on the verge of being able to reduce matters to a fairly simple formula when, deep beneath his underwear, Urticaria Productions Limited reacted to a lightly-detected danger signal and suddenly began to double the week's output of spots. His listening and tuning apparatus caught up a moment later – just in time to hear the General, in the middle of another solo, trilling:

"...Miss Valerie Waugh poses a particularly delicate problem for us..."

Jonty panicked.

He tried to shut out the Principal's voice. He wished he had eyelids on his ears, the way his eyes had. Alternatively, why wasn't there a switch somewhere to set off a mechanism for flooding his earholes with thick wax? Was it possible to go deaf at will? Should he take up Yoga?

Feeling panic was, he supposed, all right; but feeling it as much as this was ridiculous.

Now, he knew how Styles had felt in Jarrold's office!

'But, at least, I'm not trying to disappear entirely! Besides, it would arouse their suspicions. For the moment, I just want to go stone-deaf, or even – as second-best – wax-deaf!

'That's not too bloody much to ask, is it?'

He tried to concentrate his mind on controlling the glands in his ears; but he couldn't. Why should he be surprised about that?...

Even just hinting at Valerie's name, *smerzando*, in this bandful of splay-fingered wind-players was shocking enough in itself; but the General's voice continued to go up and down a scale of terrible notes! The *recitativo* was now truly frightening:

"...It must have been a week ago that Matron brought it to my notice. Naturally, we are all very worried when any of our girls feel sick; but we take especial notice of girls who feel nauseous when they awake in the mornings. For obvious reasons. In this case..."

Urticaria Limited took over in earnest...

For his second wish, Jonty wanted his body to stop feeling as if it were being dipped in and out of boiling water. It had now become an Unlimited Company: it felt like one scalding lobster-blush from head to foot.

He closed his eyes – which he now firmly believed were out on long feelers – so that he wouldn't be able to see whether or not they were watching him, wrinkling their noses in the steam.

'Why, oh why, didn't she warn me?'

She had said nothing. God, if he was going to be a father, surely any self-respecting lobster had a right to the news?

Was it right, Jonty wanted to know, that it should be announced publicly by a large fifty-eight year old virgin who wore fibre-filled bras that sagged, and was a General in the Salvation Army? And, moreover, to a group of dead-beat wind-players trying to settle a score?

It was indecent. No wonder he was on fire, ready to be served up *bene cotto!*

Now atonal, the relentless *recitativo secco* was going forward to itemize the procedure to be followed in such unfortunate cases: medical examination; informing of parents or guardians; appropriate period of absence from studies; confidentiality of all information; later re-admission – all the steps required to save College face and Government money, and to facilitate the successful completion of training.

The whole machine of structured compassion, the formidable indecency of the conspiracy, was something that Jonty felt keenly; but he could not put his finger on any good and tangible reason why he should feel so.

It was something to do with an element of wilful blindness that offended him: 'These things go on. We all know. But we must manage them AND ignore them, you see!'

Such attitudes lit red lanterns for him.

He felt inexplicably angered: it brought up an unambiguous and cathexical impulse in him; but he needed a third wish to carry it out, he knew.

He wished mightily that he could be given the courage to get up on his chair, climb from there onto the table, and with one foot on Ursuala Pettigrew's scribbling-pad, direct himself full-frontal at the Chair and yell out at the top of his lungs:

"I did it! Me! Probationer Jonty! Your Lecturer in English! I did it! And I did it with THIS!"

Thereupon, he would begin to unfasten his fly – very slowly – and watch their fascination, horror and shock empty the Music Room...

Unfortunately, Jonty hadn't got that kind of courage. It was questionable if, in such situations, he had any kind of courage:

'Suppose my zip sticks halfway down?'

But oh! how he wished he could just teach them things!...

What things?...

Well, for instance, to give them a bit of stick; make them suffer; force them to see the workings of Clatworthy's *realpolitik*; teach them what to take note of and what to ignore; not to put their tubas, euphoniums and ocarinas away in steamy conditions to tarnish, and then lament the cost of Brasso.

Most of all – TO TEACH THEM TO DAMN WELL SHUT UP!

What was the good of Clatworthy going on so long about it? And why, after going on so long, was she going on to repeat *recitativo stromentato* her list of what she was FOR and AGAINST?

Who would grant him his three wishes?

Why didn't she contract instant laryngitis, or pharyngeal hernia, or something?

WHY AM I BEING SUBJECTED TO THIS?

But he knew why...

Jonty kept his eyes on his scribbling pad.

He positively did not want to watch the purpling of her dewlaps, wobbling with indignation, as she reached the top notes. He also knew that, by now, her eyes were beginning to stick out much further than they usually did; that their glint had hardened, sweeping like a bass broom through the Music Room, prickling the faces of his colleagues, scratching round their thoughts, abrading their hysteria, and disturbing the dirt.

He began to scribble defensively on his pad. 'Think about the syllabus. Think about the syllabus.'

He muttered it over and over to himself. He covered a page with it: THINK ABOUT THE SYLLABUS.

It didn't work; so he began to write whatever came into his head, anything, as quickly as he could, just to shut out the General's unremitting *recitativo*: 'As well as studies in Emphalosophy, I propose that we add Arabic and Persian Bird Calls to the course in Far Eastern Teaching Methods and Western Technology that we are continuing to learn nothing about since last year.

'Next year, I propose that we widen the syllabus still further. Take, for example, the crucial question: Do infants in infancy get as much of it as adults in adultery? Who would hazard an answer to this?

'Therefore, I propose that we add Sex Education in the Kindergarten to the nothing we learned about it this year, and structure the whole operation as a disciplined exercise in organized ignorance. The course could be distinguished by the notable absence of Practical Work, Diagrams, Illustrations, or indeed, of Content of any intelligible kind.

'This would sort well with a number of courses already on offer; after all, the Traditions of the College Must Be Kept UP. I think we should all resolve to keep them UP. If WE don't keep them up, WHO THE BLOODY HELL ELSE WILL KEEP THEM UP?

'And I ask that advisedly... Did someone propose UPALL? Yes, I second that... WE WANT UPALL!...UP, UP, UP!... UP ALL!... UP All!'

Even then, Jonty had to go on chanting the refrain for a number of minutes after he had used all the leaves of his scribbling pad before the Honourable General, Member for Nether Prudery and Ignorance, unexpectedly finished her oratorio.

But, suddenly, it was all over.

He had weathered the storm, and they were on to the next student, as if nothing untoward had happened!

Jonty was exhausted.

What incredible powers of stamina they had! Such wonderful gifts of insensibility! Either... Both... Jonty closed his eyes and tried not to think, feel, or sense – anything!

What is the mode of no eyes watching, no ears hearing, no fingers touching?...

He regained his full awareness to the sound of coughing, chattering, the scraping of chairs and general noises of exit. He got up and followed them. Outside, in the corridor, he overheard Big Rev explaining something in his Paul Robeson voice to The Pettigrew.

"Yes, that's right! At Tolleshunt Knights in the Old Rectory... The Community do not normally eat meat. But they make a point of doing so on Easter Day... In order that they may NOT claim NEVER to eat meat... Do you see how it works, Ursula?"

As Jonty sidled into the small space left between the pair of do-gooders and a small group of biddies scratching in the doorway, he noted that the Pettigrew's eyes were a trifle glassy in her keratinized face. Big Rev had his back towards him; but somehow he was alerted, and suddenly turned to Jonty and boomed:

"Ah! Jonty! I'd like a word with you. Excuse me, Miss Pettigrew!"

Big Reverend Heffler stalked – all six foot four of him – over to a vacant space in the foyer near to one of the walls, and waited for Jonty to follow. Meekly, Jonty went across to the pastoral mountain. Big Rev peered down on Jonty from his altitude.

At that very moment, George Upall chose to go by, unseeingly – with a smile like an angel's on his face. Big Rev took the tiny ball of tightly screwed-up paper from the top pocket of his clergyman's jacket and dropped it into Jonty's palm.

"Your message," he boomed, "would appear to show a strong obsession with coprophilous matters. You have a preference for words of less than five letters, Mr Jonty, relating mainly to the processes of excretion, human and inhuman... But, next time," he threatened, *sotto voce*, "I shall be forced to go to the Principal."

He left Jonty standing where he was and walked with dignified stride back to Ursula Pettigrew.

Jonty, alive to his colleagues milling about him, but rarely embarrassed, had been mutely bound by it. This was now in his favour, together with the extravagances of the scrawled message to Upall.

Big Rev had been so shocked by the natural vulgarity of Jonty's turn of expression – its lusty swearing, its bounding lack of caution – that he had failed to connect the public exuberance of the notices appearing on the College boards with the prodigalities of Jonty's private style.

So much the better for Jonty!

But, objectively considered, whose side did God think he was on?

Didn't the genre of the *oratorium* mean anything to Him? And what about the sheer potency of the brass?

Could listening to millions of hymns sung by pious congregations with no ear for music have sent Him tone-deaf, after all?

Whatever the answers, Jonty breathed in deeply and thankfully, as if he had just come up for air after a long submersion.

Whew!

He felt humbled... Some kind of a future at St Anne's had been extended for him!

14

It had taken days for Jonty to recover his sang-froid after the Staff Meeting.

Even then, he hadn't dared to make any attempt to see Valerie until another week had gone by. But, eventually, he had plucked up the courage to send her an unsigned typewritten note that simply said: *Joe Lyons. 10.00 a.m. Saturday.*

She was waiting for him when he arrived.

Luckily, at that time in the morning, the teashop was only moderately busy.

Offering her no acknowledgment, he threaded his way carefully and circuitously round the large tiled room, giving it the once-over before deciding to cross to Valerie's table to sit with her.

Her eyes were upon him as he moved about. She was wearing oatmeal-coloured trousers, a baggy olive-coloured jerkin and no hat. She looked as fresh and easy as the April morning.

Satisfied that none of the patrons knew them, he sat down and kissed her quickly. She smiled at him and something tightened itself and relaxed in the region of his solar plexus.

"How have you been?" she asked, solicitously.

"Awful! You?" he said.

"Fine!... Why awful?"

"Why?" he echoed, incredulously. "You didn't say a word... I was in the full blast of the fan! Without protective clothing... That bloody Staff Meeting!... I've developed more hang-ups than a school cloakroom!... I'm nothing but a set of twitches held together by urticaria!... Not even a smoke-signal!"

"But I didn't know for sure. Anybody can feel sick in the morning. It could have been a bug!... It was the Matron! She would insist I went to the doctor. What could I do?"

"What did he say?"

"He couldn't be certain, either. But he thinks – two months."

"So you missed a period last month!"

"Yes."

"Why didn't you say?"

"It wasn't conclusive! Anybody can miss once or twice. It's common!... Excitement can do it. Or unaccustomed – unaccustomed – you know what I mean!"

"I know what you mean," he said, and added miserably: "Doesn't seem any point in refusing Sofia her divorce now, does there? Can't protect you any more."

"That's right. Give it to her!"

"I suppose!" he said.

Then, looking at her quickly from under lowered brows, he asked suspiciously: "You didn't plan this did you?"

She made no reply, but simply smiled at him, radiantly. He sat up and put his hands on the table in front of him.

"You didn't bloody plan this bun in the oven, did you?"

"No, but I like buns," she said, and laughed...

Jonty smiled wryly as he recollected the conversation.

He entered the old stone building in which the lawyers' chambers were situated, and climbed the gloomy narrow stairs to the solicitor's office. This was Jonty's second visit to the particular partner who was looking after his 'case': Mr Morris, a tall young man with a tuft of fair hair and a long nervous pale face, was waiting for him at the top.

"Good morning, Mr Godley," said the solicitor, offering his hand.

"Good morning, Mr Morris," said Jonty, taking it.

Jonty followed Mr Morris into his office, who then offered him a chair and a cigarette.

"I don't. Thanks!" said Jonty, accepting the one and refusing the other.

"D'you mind if I do?"

"Not at all."

The solicitor sat behind his desk, inhaling lungfuls of smoke, exhaling slowly and deeply, and then repeating the cycle, while he tried to take the measure of Jonty. They sat in silence for a while, waiting for the Enquiry Agent to arrive; the young lawyer began to talk inconsequentially about this and that, his tuft of fair hair bobbing up and down as he did so.

Jonty looked about him while Mr Morris chatted.

He seemed a nice enough chap, and it seemed a nice enough office, but it felt cramped: too full of glass-fronted cabinets, too full of files and books, with an old steel safe squatting on the floor in one corner, the desk plumb in the middle, a leather armchair (which Jonty occupied) in front of the desk, and another wooden chair with a plywood seat that looked as if it had been made specially for clients with perfectly circular backsides and curvature of the spine. It had very skinny and bandy legs.

Perhaps it had a calcium deficiency, as well?

The telephone rang. Mr Morris stubbed out his nub in a clean ashtray: the first of the day. He was obviously an abstemious but luxuriant smoker.

"Hello," said Mr Morris. A pause. "All right. Send him up!"

He put back the receiver on its cradle.

"It's the Enquiry Agent," he said.

Jonty nodded.

The agent entered the office.

Nobody said anything.

The agent was puffing and sweating slightly after the stairs: of medium height, with a round pale podgy face. He seemed to have trouble with his weight.

Mr Morris stood up and gestured him towards the empty chair.

Jonty looked critically at his behind. The shape was okay; but there was going to be a decided margin of overhang.

Jonty regarded the skinny legs of the chair with great attention as the man sat down. They didn't flinch! Mmmm! Deceptive. Like the legs on donkeys. So thin and delicate, you'd think they'd break at any time, but they never did.

Sofia's representative wore a blue serge suit that looked as if it had been tailored for him by someone who had had a lot of practice sewing mailbags.

Was he a bachelor and did his own mending – and had he himself maybe done a spell inside?

He placed a heavy briefcase – almost as overweight as himself – onto his podgy knees and opened it. He withdrew from it a sheet of lined foolscap paper, which he placed on the end of the desk, in front of him. He took out his ballpoint pen.

Only then did he glance up at Mr Morris, who was thoroughly familiar with this ritual from his many previous cases, and who had been patiently awaiting the man's signal.

"This is Mr Godley," said Mr Morris, on cue. "Mrs Godley's husband."

The Enquiry Agent acknowledged Jonty with the briefest of nods.

Jonty guessed that he did not lean against the back of the chair because he knew from past experience about its flair for inducing scoliosis in the sitter.

"Hello," said Jonty.

The man did not reply.

"Now," said Mr Morris "remember, *I'm* here as an observer only. You two go ahead."

Jonty looked at the Solicitor in surprise

'Go ahead what? Does he think I want to dance with this Herbert?'

"Have you any means of identification?" asked the agent abruptly.

Jonty looked back at the Agent. He looked again at Mr Morris. Mr Morris was examining his fingernails. Jonty felt hustled. He turned to the agent.

"No," he said, after a long pause.

"How do I know that you are the man Mr Morris tells me you are?" said the agent, at once.

Jonty appealed yet again to Mr Morris, who shrugged his shoulders, picked up a file from his desk and began to peruse it.

'Oh! Like that, is it?' thought Jonty.

He settled himself back comfortably in the leather armchair. If it was going to be a struggle, he might as well enjoy it!

"Well, you don't, do you?" said Jonty, affably. "You'll have to take it on faith."

"Faith!" snorted the man, and laughed cynically, trying to throw his head rearwards as he did so; but he was prevented by the chins he had rolled to the back of his neck.

"Have you got a photograph of yourself?" he shot out, recovering himself nicely.

"Don't use them!" said Jonty. "What about you?"

"Me?" asked the man, blankly.

Jonty waited a moment before replying.

"Yes. You!... How do I know you are the man you tell me you are?"

It was the agent's turn to look across the desk at Mr Morris, who had his nose deep in the file.

"You may be an impostor for all I know," went on Jonty.

The agent turned to face him.

Jonty continued:

"I don't even know your name!... Have YOU got a photograph of yourself to show?... What about my wife – did she give you a letter of introduction to me?... Where are YOUR bloody *bona fides*?" he ended stridently.

"I'm only doing my job, Mr Godley," said the agent, plaintively.

"Ah! so now you admit I'm Godley!" said Jonty, quick as a ferret down a rabbit-hole.

"No! I don't admit anything," wailed the agent. "You might be PRETENDING to be Mr Godley."

"I see! The Young Pretender!... You think I'm trying to get a divorce from somebody else's wife?"

"No! But I've got to prove to the judge that I've interviewed the right man! Don't make things difficult for me, Mr Godley!" said the agent, peevishly.

"Why not? That's what you're doing for me, isn't it?" asked Jonty, belligerently. "For all I know, YOU could be impersonating an Enquiry Agent. That's perjury!... Look here, you're not Sofia's lover, are you?" he asked suddenly, sitting forward in his chair to peer up at the man.

Beads of sweat began to glisten round the agent's temples. He looked baffled. Mr Morris put his head deeper into his file.

"Why should I do that?" he asked, lamely.

"Exactly!" hooted Jonty, in triumph, and leaned back in his armchair.

"Mr Godley," said the man, imploringly. "don't you have ANY means of identification?"

"What about a driving licence?"

The agent's face brightened.

"Do you have a Driving Licence?"

"If I have – how do you know I haven't found it? Or stolen it?"

"Yes, I suppose you're right," said the agent glumly. "Possession would be no proof that it's yours."

"You see!" said Jonty triumphantly, uncertain about what he wanted the man to see.

But by now, it had become a game: parry and thrust, feint and punch.

"I've never had trouble like this before," complained the agent.

"That's because you've never divorced a Godley before," said Jonty, happily.

"All right!" said the man. "I'll accept the Driving Licence."

"I haven't got one!"

"Mr Godley, you're not helping me at all! If you want to get your divorce, you'll have to help me."

"Who said I wanted one? My wife wants it. If I want it as well, that's collusion, isn't it?... Am I SUPPOSED to help you?"

"No, you're not!... But don't you want a divorce?"

"Don't answer that, Mr Godley!" put in Mr Morris at great speed, without lifting his head out of the file.

"All right!" said the agent, wearily. "Let's get on to other matters. When did you first see Miss Waugh?"

"Can't remember."

"Well – roughly?"

"About the end of last year."

"Let's see! That's six or seven months ago, isn't it?"

"Near enough."

"Where?"

"Where what?"

"Where did you first see her?"

"I saw her in one of my classes."

The agent looked dully at Jonty, his ballpoint poised over his notebook.

"She's a student at the college I work in," Jonty explained.

"Oh, I see."

He wrote it down.

"When was the first occasion sexual intercourse took place?" he asked, without looking up, in a matter-of-fact tone of voice; but the question surprised Jonty, all the same.

He saw a wet car park and two figures walking gingerly across the glistening tarmac, the girl very carefully, like a blind thing: it flashed on, a slide on a screen. Then it went off. His feelings soared.

"I don't remember," he said.

"Oh?"

"Wouldn't the last occasion do?" asked Jonty.

The man put on an expression of bafflement again, which he was very good at. It was, clearly, one of the tools of his trade.

"All right," he said, as if beaten.

Jonty told him and the man scribbled it in his notebook.

"During the period you have known Miss Waugh, have you had sexual intercourse regular?"

It was Jonty's turn to laugh. He laughed.

"It all depends on what you mean by 'regular', don't it?" asked Jonty, ungrammatically entering into the spirit of the thing.

Mr Morris's eyes flickered up and down, in and out of his file, and his tuft of fair hair quivered slightly.

"Well – regular is regular," said the man, his eyes glued to his notebook, still writing.

"Once a year? Once a week? Once a night? Four times a day?... Have you read Kinsey's 'Report on the Sexual Behaviour of the Human Male?'... How would you define 'regular'?... I could be a new Folk Hero!"

"Would it be fair to state," asked the man, with ponderous patience, looking steadfastly at Mr Morris, who ignored him, "that it took place whenever you and your partner had the opportunity?"

"Fair, but not accurate," replied Jonty.

"How'd you mean?"

He looked up at Jonty, quickly.

"Well, if you must know, we had it sometimes when we didn't have the opportunity! Or the time. Only the inclination."

"I see."

The agent began writing again.

"And very embarrassing it was, too!" added Jonty.

"I don't think we need to go into that," said the agent.

"I beg your pardon!" said Jonty, with heavy irony. "I was only trying to be exact."

"Yes, I appreciate that, Mr Jonty. But the judge wouldn't.... So, what shall I put down then?"

"Why not write: 'It took place at weekends, whenever Miss Waugh got off from College?' Won't that help?"

"What about this?" asked the agent.

He held up his notebook in front of him and read laboriously: "'I met Miss Waugh at a Teacher's Training College in Colchester last year. We went out together soon after. Sexual intercourse took place whenever possible.' Will that do?"

"Oh, yes! 'Whenever possible' instead of 'whenever opportune'. Very deft! I like that!... On the whole."

The agent looked slightly mollified by Jonty's remarks.

"But – libellous!" added Jonty.

His face sweated emptily. "How'd you mean – libellous?"

"Well – listen to it! 'Intercourse took place whenever possible'."

"Sounds all right to me!"

"Oh, you approve, do you?"

Before the man could object, Jonty said: "Makes me sound impotent, don't it?"

"That's not what I meant, Mr Jonty."

"As long as the judge—"

"—Could you give me some idea of the address you live at, Mr Jonty?"

'Shall I describe the cellar to him, or tell him about the bathroom?'

"What kind of an idea?" Jonty asked aloud.

"What?... Well, the road and number!"

Jonty told him. The agent wrote it down. He wrote it down wrongly and had to erase it and do it again.

'God knows what it's all going to sound like when he's finished putting it through his shredder!' thought Jonty.

The agent soon stopped asking questions. Jonty was relieved. Mr Morris was still deep in his file. Jonty watched the agent re-writing his confession on to the sheet of foolscap paper on the desk. He did not write quickly. When he had finished, he handed it to Jonty to read. It was written in a semi-literate, pseudo-legal and highly stylized English.

"It makes me sound as if I've just escaped from an Institution!" objected Jonty.

"Just sign it at the bottom, if you don't mind, Mr Godley," said the agent, smoothly.

"What about all the mistakes and alterations?"

"You have to sign them as well."

"What for?"

"To prove I haven't forged it."

"Forged it!... Well, I suppose it does take a special kind of genius to invent mistakes like these!"

"Just so, Mr Godley! Sign it right there, please."

Jonty signed it.

The agent folded the foolscap sheet with undisguised satisfaction and put it into his lumpy briefcase. He spent a long time fastening it.

Only afterwards did he remove his bottom from the circular seat of the chair and shake hands, first with Jonty and then with Mr Morris.

"Good morning, gentlemen," he said tonelessly, and went out.

Jonty and Mr Morris were left looking at each other. There was a half-smile on the young man's face.

"Sorry about all this," said Mr Morris, jerking his head in the direction taken by the agent, so that his coif bobbed. "Necessary, I'm afraid; but it makes the whole thing sound like a sordid mistake, or even like taking out a contract on somebody's life. If you see what I mean?"

"Yes. I know. Though, to me, it felt more like a bloodless and fatal accident!... Maybe, this is how it feels to be dead?" added Jonty.

"Yes. It's a sad way to end a marriage," said Mr Morris.

"Yes," said Jonty, chastened.

"So I'll see you in due course," said Mr Morris. "Keep well," he said, holding out his hand.

Jonty took it.

"See you," he said. "And thanks."

As he left the building, he felt chilled, although it was a warm April day.

He walked back along the High Street, towards Joe Lyons' Teashop where he had left Valerie and wondered why it was that sadness somehow made him feel anonymous and cold. He felt as if some of his individuality had waned, as if the flame of his self had been darkened, the fuel drained away and replaced with thin flakes of ice, packed carefully, as if in a tiny battery, deep inside him. He knew if he waited too long alone, he would become such a flake himself; he would begin to whirl, directionless, in a storm of such flakes, losing himself... as he remembered doing once before, after leaving his father in the hospital, and becoming extinguished, faceless, a nullity...

Valerie! That was the answer. He hurried towards her.

She was still sitting at the same table in the tea-rooms, alone, although the place was now fairly full of people. Regardless of caution, he went straight to her and held her. She responded at once. He sat down, already feeling better.

"What happened?" she asked.

"The bloody agent wanted me to show him a photograph – of me, to prove that I WAS me!"

"What!"

"Yes, ridiculous, isn't it? I asked him to show me one of him to prove that HE was him."

"Did he?"

"No! So we never got introduced."

Valerie laughed.

"Tell me about it!"

"I will! But we'll get tea, first! By then, I might even feel up to drinking it. Genteely, of course!

"How's that?"

"With two fingers in the air!... No, not those two!... I mean the index and the pinkie!"

In the warmth of her presence, he began to regain himself...

That had been several weeks ago. Not long after the episode of the Enquiry Agent, Valerie left St Anne's discreetly, and after placating her mother, moved in with Jonty. They had taken good care that nobody at the college knew where she went.

Her mother had agreed to allow the College authorities to think that Valerie was under her care. Luckily, Valerie's mother liked Jonty; she could see that he wanted to take care of her daughter, and that Valerie needed him in return.

Mrs Waugh was a canny soul.

It was a Friday morning that happened to be free of lectures for Jonty, who was at home; Valerie had gone shopping.

As he sat at the long kitchen table, working on yet another revision of the syllabus for Miss Clatworthy's cherished English Course, watching rain fall in a steady pitch-stained stream into the bucket in the middle of the kitchen floor, he mused on the fact that, during the last few months of their living together, he had scarcely had a chance to assess things – a routine as necessary as breathing to Jonty.

Was it the silent process of growth and decay going on around him that made him realize this?

Every so often, a drop of rain would miss the bucket, having come out further along the crack in the ceiling, and would drip, hissing, onto the hot iron stove that warmed the kitchen, shatter, and run off the glowing plate in tiny lucid beads of quicksilver. Trifling pieces of whitewash detached themselves from the ceiling and wavered up and down in the heat that rose from the stove. From time to time, a fragment of yellow emulsion (Mr Bennet's sunshine) would flake from the wall and flutter to the floor.

The heat accelerated the flaking; the rain and damp hastened the cracking that was forever going on.

In some way he found difficult to analyze, they seemed like emblems, elusive, but expressive of insights that were valuable to him. Was it because everything was part of the same cycle, a unity of quickening and growing and decaying and falling away?

Was that it?

Of late, he had been feeling hurried and harried . He wished that a lot that had happened over the last year had not happened at all; in any case, events should not have been crammed into periods of time that were too small, or even inappropriate to them.

For example, what had Father Time thought he was doing a year ago by making room for that stroke of purest bastardy: slotting him into an interview for a job in a women's Training College? If the Old Dotard had taken the trouble to step to one side at the right moment, Jonty would not have been in that place with those people at that time, would he?

Time was supposed to be on the side of youth, wasn't it?

Why did it feel as if it wasn't, if it was?

Of course, making room for Valerie to happen to him had been marvellous! There was no disputing that. It had been a stroke of sheerest ingenuity!

But the Old Guy had let what happened afterwards happen too bloody fast, not to say, precipitously.

Valerie pregnant!

Jonty had not expected that particular swish of the scythe. Until then, Jonty had worked on the basic assumption that what you expected to happen, for the most part, happened; what you did not expect to happen, rarely did.

He was wrong, wasn't he?

Quite clearly, if the Old Buffer felt like a quick careless slash, you could find yourself standing without a leg to stand on. Precipitous!

"Good word that. Precipitous!" he said, to himself.

Perhaps it had all turned out for the best? But if the Old Buffer had betrayed him, may his scythe rust in the morning dews and need honing every fifteen seconds, or less!

With that satisfying thought, Jonty went back to redrafting Miss Clatworthy's English Syllabus (New Version).

15

But Jonty could not keep his mind on the new English syllabus. His feeling of crowded leglessness kept pushing it away and moving it in another direction. Something – what was it? – just insisted on being considered. After trying for some time to concentrate on prescribed books, Jonty gave in, and let his mind meander where it would: it turned to Clatworthy, The Pettigrew, and Big Rev.

In his daydream, they seemed to have linked arms and were striding three-abreast, Forwards and Onwards, with Courage and Faith to the Illimitable and Expanding Horizon of Bastardy that stretched before them… Then came Spring, with the odour of Urticaria Pigmentosa heavy on the air... On the whole, Jonty felt that it was a season he could have done without.

Why couldn't Winter have gone on up until Summer this year, just for a change? It wouldn't have been the first time...

Meanwhile the terrible trio went relentlessly forward into the middle distance, trampling underfoot anybody who got in their way. Jonty saw himself scampering ahead of them, breathlessly being driven towards the evil-smelling pit he had eventually fallen into at that grisly Staff Meeting.

Condescendingly, they had stopped to smile down at him from its edge, as he tried to keep himself from going completely under, where they intoned a chorus about something else going on – in a different time-scale, an evolutionary one – inside a Miss Waugh. Then, with a brief gesture of dismissal to Valerie, they strode onwards, confident of Success, leaving him to flounder.

As a fitting climax had come the Enquiry Agent fiasco.

HE was something from a different evolutionary scale, all right; in retrospect, thought Jonty, he seemed like something you woke up sweating about, after a heavy meat-meal, eaten just before bedtime.

Although, on consideration, he had survived that particular nightmare pretty well at the time, hadn't he?... And how did it come about that the whole crowded sequence, the kaleidoscopic speed of the happenings, seemed to have occurred alongside a terrible sparseness of beer: a positive drought of it, in fact?

At this point in his reveries, Jonty experienced a sudden injection of reality: How could you explain being able to feel that you were lost in a beerless desert AND, at one and the same time, in a genteel suburb of crowded bastardy? How is it that the feeling you were being jostled and harried and pursued did not exclude the feeling that you were being quiet and solitary and pensive, while you watched pitch-coloured rainwater drip into a bucket?

Hey?

He sighed deeply, not knowing why he sighed, and looked about him.

Of course, it hadn't all been change for the worse. A lot of the harassment and haste had been taken out of life by the routine that Valerie adopted in the house.

Look at that stove!

All the old red flaking rust had been rubbed off, and in its place was a shiny garment of black enamel. The long wooden table actually had a cloth covering it, with a tin jug of flowering snarfia in the centre that Jonty had purloined from the Public Park, up the road.

All the scurf that fell from the silently floundering house each day was swiftly disposed of; the kitchen was regularly aerosolled and the silver fish had migrated speedily to next door; even the snails, at nights in the back yard, seemed to have dropped to half-strength.

And Valerie's tea!

Not only was Jonty surprised to find he could actually drink it, but astonished to find that he liked it. None of Sofia's Mark I, II and III rubbish! No more toast, black round the edges and pale in the middle, like an African 's arsehole! It came to the table, even and golden and hotly buttered.

It was delicious like all that she cooked!

Like everything she cleaned, dusted, folded, washed and ironed.

It was marvellous!

The question was: Was Valerie like that because she had been to a Housecraft & Needlework College; or had she been to one of them because she was like that?

Those twats at the College would claim to know the answer to that one; Jonty didn't.

What was even more astonishing about Valerie was the neatness and compactness in herself; in her feelings, in her lovemaking. She had no internal spaces to stuff up with clutter. Her feelings went right up to the sides, edges and corners of her psyche; they filled the very soul of her. There was no room for dither and dust; they were full and clean and whole.

It was such a fine tasty fare!

Jonty loved the way that sex happened between them: it was unhurried and with no desperation. It grew, and they became filled with it; and when she'd had enough of it, she'd had enough.

Not like Alex – who could never have enough of it.

Not like Sofia – who didn't mind partaking, even when she'd had enough; or, for that matter, NOT partaking when she hadn't had enough; although it was enjoyed well enough, at the time.

It was novel, making love to Valerie; it was strange; it was nice. She actually seemed to know what she wanted; and when, where and how she wanted it. He loved her honesty about it, her practicality, her psychological competence.

He loved also the fullness with which, from day to day, her being was filled, the juice of a correct and discriminating compassion that made her lush.

And best and most incredible in his eyes, it all seemed to add up to one little nonsensical word: Jonty.

What a thing! Jonty!

What a funny bloody thing it was! Fancy wanting a Jonty, actually wanting one of your own! And it was funny the way a Valerie wanting a Jonty made a Jonty wanting a Valerie seem so important and so nice. It was completely satisfying.

Why?

And the way it made you feel different about a spot of the other. Funny!

Of course, a spot of that had always been all right; there had been enough point in doing it for its own sake to keep him normally happy.

Wasn't he like everybody else?

Of course, he was!

But with Valerie, it was different; he didn't just do it for its own sake; it wasn't just wedging a quim. In a sense, naturally, it was still that, too: but that was the unavoidable side-effect of actually wedging a quim, wasn't it?

Did that make sense?

Of course, it did!

Especially when you added the incredible marvellousness of wedging *this* particular quim to the *usual* side-effect-marvellousness of quim-wedging in general; *and* you remembered that, together, they made the whole experience into something so much better than any experience of sex he had been able to imagine.

See?

I'm not sure.

Well, if you're not sure, I am.

I know what I mean.

And I know what I like. And THAT'S what I like.

If you can't find the words for it, who cares? It's still there, isn't it?'

Jonty's speculations had exasperated him.

He had not been able to catch the elusiveness, the aliveness of the experiences he was trying to analyze. It always annoyed him when he failed.

'But, maybe it's all right to be a Pisces?... By the by, what's Valerie's sign?'

He realized he didn't know. He must remember to ask her when she got back from her shopping.

Jonty looked dubiously at the sheets of paper on the table in front of him. He knew that he HAD to work on the new syllabus – which he had promised to hand in by the beginning of next week.

But, this morning, he wasn't able to keep his mind on his task. It seemed a logical enough step, in his present mood, to go from George Eliot to The Pettigrew, and from there to acknowledging that she disliked him enough to ask him to tea, and from thence to wondering why she disliked him SO MUCH... and to wondering whether The Pettigrew had been a spinster since infancy... and thence to wondering if she had actually been had by parents, as it was alleged everybody had been had by; or if, like Topsy, she had just growed...

Twaggin had been interesting on spinsters. "A contented spinster is a contradiction in terms," he had said.

Good old Twaggin!

He'd thought about everything and experienced nothing – or nearly nothing.

Not that that invalidated what he said, not at all.

He was so damn perceptive!

Experience, he would get; we all did...

Of course, it was important to remember that the term 'spinster' covered both sexes, as Twaggin had so often reminded him; and to remember that their life-cycles were marked by an absence of childhood, youth, or old age, which was another way of saying that they were deficient in the essential dimensions of the heart.

What about The Pettigrew? Had she ever wanted to get married? Be made love to?...

George Upall had once said that he doubted if she would ever come across anybody public-spirited enough to have a shot at it!

Would she ever?

What was her discontent with, and dislike of, Jonty linked to?

Perhaps against all the odds – give her the benefit of the doubt! – she had actually had a childhood, and been frightened by a Jonty-like father in the process?...

Maybe it was all a matter of scent? Perhaps he didn't emit the right electrons?... Was she in love with Big Rev?...

Jonty had to admit that The Pettigrew baffled him.

He simply couldn't fathom what made her tick; and this vexed him. He couldn't, for the life of him, understand why it should: he only knew that he had to try to understand her, as he had tried to understand the Reverend F.E. Newey, and others – simply, because they were there.

Some instinct told him that The Pettigrew was the kind of reader who wrote anonymously about her problems to the 'Lonely Hearts' columns of women's magazines; and perhaps Jonty, as an avid reader of them, could help himself to grasp her if he wrote a letter – the kind he hoped she would be able to write – on her behalf? That is, if she'd actually been an adolescent at some time or other – which was doubtful; and if she had had normal urges, which was—

Oh, to hell with it! Here goes!

Dear Aunty Doris, My boyfriend refuses to kiss me. He says it's old-fashioned. He's got other ideas. But I won't let him. I think it's because I keep getting my nose in the way. I don't want to lose him, because this is the fourth time it's happened. But it might be my thick ankles. Or more likely my acne.

What I want to know is would professional plastic surgery be worth the time and money?

Yours sincerely,

Acne-Sufferer.

That seemed to take care of fidelity to The Pettigrew's physical characteristics, all right, especially her keratinized complexion. But was it faithful to her keratinized psychology? Could she have really written a pathetic letter like that?

He sighed. He hoped for her sake she could have.

If only people like her would let themselves be seen naked, or half-clothed, once in a while; give someone a chance to have a qood squint at her vulnerability, now and then. How much nicer she would be! Instead of wrapping herself up in that thick-weave humility, that loud-check chastity, and that brand of powdered do-goodery she actually favoured.

Pity!

Sorrowfully, Jonty took up his pencil to write Aunty's reply:

Dear Acne-Sufferer,

Yes.

Yours ever,

Aunty Doris.

He simply couldn't do any more for Ursula Pettigrew, could he? He had gone to the limit of his sympathy for her and now he was stymied...

For God's sake, get back to the syllabus!

It was at that point he heard Valerie returning from her shopping. He was glad about that. It gave him an excuse to stop getting back to the syllabus, and he was glad about that, also.

She came into the kitchen, from the passageway, with her purchases. The rain sparkled on her long dark cape. Her eyes were bright and happy. She put down the bags, and said: "Again it kicked! It kicked!"

"What did?"

"The baby, you idiot! A little thump. Right here!"

She opened her cape and placed her hand on her right side.

"You sure it wasn't the twinges of an incipient appendicitis, or something?"

"Of course! It was him, all right."

"Him?"

"All right! Her! A real foot, now, not just a little bud! Isn't it marvellous?"

"Let's feel!"

Jonty got up from the table, went across to her and placed his hand tenderly on the spot she had indicated.

"Whew!"

"What's the matter?" she said in alarm.

"Size 13, at least!"

"Idiot! It's stopped now. I'll tell you when it happens again."

Valerie took off her cape, shook it, and hung it on the hook behind the door. Jonty watched her with appreciation.

If that had been Sofia, she'd have rested it across the butter.

"It's stopped raining," said Valerie. "And I've been thinking. We need a cot."

"Are those two statements connected?" asked Jonty. Valerie ignored him, so he went on: "There's a month or two before then, isn't there? What do you–?"

"—I know! But I like to be prepared."

"I see... Patrol Leader in the Scouts, were you?"

She didn't answer.

Jonty said: "Come to think of it, I saw something that looked like a cot downstairs – in old Bennet's cellar!"

"Oooh! Horrible! We couldn't use that!"

"No! It wasn't horrible! A real Victorian heirloom, it looked. A boxshaped thing, on big rockers, painted curlicues. We could do it up!"

"Do you think so?"

"Yes, I think so!... And I could start practising with it – to become a Victorian Patriarch. Shall I grow a beard?"

"I know the kind you mean! They rock every time the baby moves! That would be nice, wouldn't it? Okay! Show me!"

They went out of the kitchen and into the passageway. Under the marble stairway was a door leading down into the cellar. They went gingerly down the steep stone steps.

"Isn't it dark?" said Valerie.

"Stay where you are!" said Jonty. "There's a switch somewhere. Wait a minute!... There!"

The cellar flooded with light, washing up heavy shadows in lumps and folds in the corners and over the heaped objects.

"What a jumble!" exclaimed Valerie.

"Old Bennet's proud of this cellar. He brought me down here, when I first came to inspect the place."

The junk was stacked in some kind of order: mildewed books, enormous gilt picture-frames without pictures, gas-meters (why gas-meters?), cracked and half-assembled Roman pottery, tea-chests full of old clothes, coal dust, and various pieces of furniture.

"It's like the inside of Doris Crawford's head down here. I like it!" said Jonty.

"What's he want those pots for?"

"Amateur archaeology! Colchester's full of it! Old Roman site. He sticks them together and sells them to the museums. He tells me he's good at it."

"But isn't it AWFUL, here?"

"Yes, in a way! But all his instincts are the other way."

"How do you mean?" asked Valerie, uneasily. "The other way?"

"See that chair with three legs?"

"Where?... That? Yes."

"Well, the first time I saw it, it was tipped over, fallen on the floor. When he spotted it, he stood it upright with a smile of satisfaction. He tries to be tidy!"

She cast her professional eye over the cellar.

"Might as well try and get a polish on solid darkness!" she said, derisively.

Jonty laughed.

"Well, it's like the whole house! That knocker – Leo, the lion! The sarcophagus! It's pure Bennet!"

That was another attribute that Jonty loved: Valerie SAID things.

"I'll tell you something else he mentioned on that first occasion. 'When prospective women tenants come' – he's got a deep voice like this! – 'if I bring them down here, they think I'm going to murder them, and hang them up on those hooks!'"

Jonty laughed at the recollection. Valerie looked upwards, over her head.

"Which hooks?"

"No, not there! Over there! Near the corner."

He pointed to three huge rusty hooks, fastened into the ceiling joists, partly obscured by the piled-up tea-chests. Valerie looked dubiously at them without speaking.

"Then old Bennet hung on them by his huge hands," said Jonty, going across to them. "And let his head loll. Like this," he said, imitating a hanged man. "Very lifelike, it was!"

"He was trying to be bizarre!...He sounds nice!"

"He is!" said Jonty, letting the hooks go. He pointed across to the opposite corner.

"Look, there it is! What do you think?"

She threaded her way amongst the junk to where she could crane and peer at the cot. She reached out with her hand and rocked it. A little smile played around her lips, to be erased at once when she saw the dust on her palm.

"Mmmm! I think it'll do," she said at last.

Jonty was relieved: new cots were expensive. He looked at her, where she stood. She had a strange expression on her face.

"What's the matter?" he asked, vaguely disturbed.

"Quick, Arnold! Feel! It's doing it again."

Jonty went and stood at her back. She reached behind her, took his hands and wrapped them around her. He let his palm rest gingerly where she had placed it. In a moment, he felt a sharp little jerk under his hand. Swiftly, he took his hand away from her and looked intently into his palm.

"Why, the little bugger!" he said in delight.

"Feel it?" she asked, excitedly.

"Is that it? Is it now over? Is that the full performance?"

"Yes! It's only a twitch. Just now and then."

"That wasn't a twitch. That was a good solid placekick, at least!"

They both laughed with the wonder and delight of it. He stood with his hands on her stomach, while she leaned back on him, her hair thick and lush under his chin.

"Your geography's changing fast," he said.

"Of course!" she said, proudly.

"You used to be a half-inch contour map in pastel colours."

"What am I now?" she asked, half-turning her head.

"An eight-inch relief map in strong greens and browns."

"Well, go away, if you don't like it!" she said, moving slightly forward of his body, not fancying his comparison very much.

"I like it!... I love it. Don't move!"

She relaxed against him again. Her middle bulged under his hands. He loved the way she carried it – neat, and full as an egg.

She lay in his arms like that, too; or swept up the house; or put on her bra.

No wonder he had compared her in the classroom to a ballerina, enchanting the Hooded Crusher and his mates. Every contour of her body was economical, compact and rhythmic, like a figure in a dance; unlike, in that it was not only expressive of, existing by and for itself, but there to convey some fundamental insight about her to him.

Only, he couldn't say what the insight was, exactly: it seemed so much a part of her that he couldn't separate it from what and how she was in the flesh. The way she moved, the ebb and flow of her contours, the way she seemed to be contained and filled in by her psyche, her feelings, her body, WAS the insight. The constituent parts added up to a metaphor that, as it were, expressed her self completely to him.

Did he do that for her? Was he making sense? Did it matter if he wasn't, as long as HE knew how he felt about HER?

He nuzzled her ear-lobes with his mouth.

"They're just the kind YOU should have, and taste just the way they SHOULD," he said.

"Stop it! It makes my knees feel weak. What a place to do this in!"

"Let's go to bed, then," said Jonty, at once.

"All right. But not to stay there until tomorrow morning!"

"Why not?"

"Because there's a lot of today left!... And I thought it would be nice to go and see your father... Besides, tomorrow is Guy Fawkes night. They'll be lighting bonfires and setting off fireworks."

"We can start our own conflagration in bed."

"Don't you want to see your Pa?" asked Valerie.

"AND fireworks!... Anyway, it's raining!"

"I told you: it's stopped... I love fireworks! Shall we go, Arnold?"

"To bed?"

"Yes! No!... You know what I mean!"

"Okay! But afterwards, a long time afterwards," he said, holding her to him. "Tomorrow."

"Tomorrow!"

She jerked herself away from him in surprise.

"Yes; we can't go today. I've got to finish this bloody syllabus for Monday! Remember? Anyway, the trains wouldn't be right for today. We'd arrive at some godforsaken hour in the early morning."

"All right, then!" she said, satisfied. "You've persuaded me."

"Oh, yes! I've just remembered," he said, "Are you a Pisces, by any chance?"

"Let's go to bed, and you can find out," she said.

16

"That was marvellous! I feel it's clearing up my Urticaria, nicely."

"Do you think it could?"

"Why not? Every time, I feel a few more spots pack up and steal away!"

She squeezed his arm and let him guide her along the platform and out of the station. Not many people travelled on November the Fifth, by train, on a Saturday afternoon and evening, that was clear.

They had had a carriage to themselves – of the variety with no corridor – for the whole journey. Stretched along the seat, between Coventry and Birmingham, with her back to the engine, Jonty had made love to her again... Now, emerging from New Street Station, they felt a special link binding them; and as they walked along Station Street to the Midland Red bus stop on the Solihull route, they both felt that life was good.

The bus arrived and they boarded it. The journey was quiet and uneventful; neither felt a need for much talk. Jonty looked out of the windows at the bursts of the bonfires between the houses as the bus went on its way, and at the distant sudden spurts as new ones were lighted.

Valerie, being night-blind, was satisfied to think her thoughts and sit contentedly at his side.

For Jonty, the night and the relish of their lovemaking merged, and he felt the brightness spurting into the dark, where the darkness was alive.

Eventually, the bus jerked to a halt. It was their stop. He helped her down from the platform.

"Watch! One, two, down! That's it!"

She took his arm and let him guide her. Jonty looked around him at the opulent gardens. Under the carbon lamps, the trees were insipid and bare, but there was a feeling of growing and energy about.

"Smell the smoke!" he said.

"Feel the wind!" she said.

"See that rocket?"

"Where?... No!"

"There!"

He pointed. "Up and over... Sploosh!"

"I wish I could see properly!" she said.

"You can!"

"I mean, in the dark."

"Maybe more lovemaking will cure it. We can try switching the lights off."

"Don't be ridiculous! It won't increase the rods. Or is it the cones?"

"I know one rod it will increase," he said; but before she could reply to his innuendo, he went on: "It doesn't make me feel at all tired. What about you? Upall reckons it knackers him every time. I feel like a thousand grammes of vitamin E."

"Doctors reckon it's equivalent to a five-mile walk."

"How'd you mean – equivalent? Nothing like that happens at the end of my walks."

"The energy used, silly!... Oh, it WAS good! When it's right, it makes you want to dance, doesn't it?"

"I usually sit out at dances, or go to the bar. But I know what you mean... May I have the next foxtrot?" he asked, turning to her and bowing, very formally.

"Certainly! I thought you'd never ask. Excuse my lump, won't you?"

They began to dance along the roadway.

"I can't see!"

"Don't worry! Follow me! I'm following the chap in front."

They whirled and turned and sidestepped, round and round, until they were breathless. They stopped and laughed happily.

Bangers and crackers were going off in the gardens about them. Rockets went high up into the night sky. Cats ran spitting into bushes and corners. Dogs, their tails between their legs, skulked behind dustbins.

"You know what?" asked Jonty.

"No! What?"

"I bet General Clatworthy and The Pettigrew are out with Big Rev, in a barrow. 'Penny for the guy, sir! Penny for the guy!'"

"No! Not them. They're huddled round a small packet of sparklers in the College kitchens!"

"I'd love to set fire to one of their gussets! Think of all those dummies, full of stuffing! Think of all their puddings, spices and cake mixtures! You'd never smell a bonfire like that again! The appetising odour of roasting prejudice! The ribs of conformity, done to a turn! Ah! What a lovely smell! What a blaze that would be!"

"They're not as bad as all that!"

"You're not backing out on me now, are you? What are they as bad as, then? They threw you out, didn't they?"

"Well, why not? They've got no facilities for having babies, have they?" she asked reasonably.

"True! Nor facility!... But thrown out WITH a dishonourable mention! They built up an impressive head of indignation over it; it came hissing out of their valves and stuffing-boxes, like the steam of the Satanic Mills... Deafening!"

"Oh, this wind!" she said, holding her hands in the air, and whirling around in a pirouette. "I love it! I love the wind. Through my hair like this. The smell of Autumn and smoke!"

"See that!" said Jonty.

A fountain of red-eyed sparks fanned up and out, into the air, behind the dark bulk of a house.

"Where?... There?... Oh, I do wish I could see properly!" she said in exasperation, coming to rest. "Damn this, damn this!"

The red sparks paused, and blackened one by one, falling and fallen.

"Another poor guy tossed into the flames!" said Jonty.

Anonymous shouts from the vicinity of the bonfire unwound themselves like streamers on the wind and the heat:

"Watch out!"

"Run!"

"Wheeee! Look at it go!"

As they walked through the night, again sedately, tattered bits of words, and little neat round noises, like confetti, floated into the dark, and incomprehensible showers of cries flew up to the night sky.

"I loved Bonfire Night, even when I was very young," said Valerie. "I love it now. It's a lovely half-seen world – colours and – oh! I don't know – no shape, and every shape, somehow... I think I love it because I can only see it in snatches. Little glimpses. With my silly eyes, it's a world I'll never see properly... Oh, I can't explain! I just love it. Don't you, Arnold?"

"Yeah, it turns me on, man! That Guy Fawkes had got sump'n goin' fer him."

"Don't talk like that, Arnold!" Valerie said sharply. "That half-language! It's awful!"

"Listen to her!... Folks, let me introduce you to the NEW Mrs Grundy."

"I know it sounds like that! But, honest, I can't bear it. It reminds me of some of the kids I had to teach... Where are we?"

"We're nearly there, love. As soon as we see three flaming balls of fire, we've arrived... But I doubt if we'll see any bonfires and fireworks in his garden," he added, as an afterthought.

"Why not?"

"He thinks they're nasty plebeian things – fireworks! And bonfires! The bread-and-circuses syndrome!"

"Oh, Arnold! Does he? Does he, really? What a shame! And I love them so much. I must be a Pleb, then!"

"I think he's afraid of them!"

"What? The bonfires?"

"Yes!"

"Afraid! Why?"

"I dunno! It's just a feeling I have about a feeling I think he has. Can't explain why!"

Sure enough, when they arrived outside the walls of the large plot of ground on which stood his father's house, the night had dimmed and deepened. The cries of the children they had heard all along the road now sounded far away, glottal and muffled in a dark throat. Over the hunched backs of the houses and their bony trees, the bonfires seemed to have paled to smoky flushes on the night sky.

However, the natural potency and panache of the three golden spheres above his father's gateway did their best to redress the balance.

Jonty stood below them and held up his arms in a ritualistic gesture of respect.

"I give you – the Fertility of the Jontys! Ta-ra! The Symbols at Your Door!" he announced. "Except – two are missing."

"What? Missing?... I can't see!"

"Never mind! You'll see them tomorrow morning. Take my word for it. They're up there, somewhere!"

He took her hand again.

"Come on, my love!"

They walked along the drive, lined with leafless lime-trees, round the back of the house to the conservatory, with all its windows dark,

170

and Jonty put his hands against the glass to peer inside. He could see nothing, except the faint outline of the partly-opened stable-top of the huge kitchen door, which led in off the conservatory.

"Let's go in," he said.

"Isn't it locked?"

"It's never locked."

Jonty opened the frame-glass door and entered. It was hot and stuffy under the glass.

"I slept in here for a while," he said.

"Smells as though it needs one of those all-over fragrances!" said Valerie.

"How right you are! I caught greenfly and blackspot in here."

"You didn't!... Where?"

"Daren't tell you! Unmentionable places!"

"Arnold, you're a fool!"

"I know."

They could see the pale-bluish electronic flickerings of a television screen reflected on the surface of the partly-opened kitchen door, and hear the subdued gitter of a lot of Received Pronunciation trying to get itself more generally received throughout the kingdom.

"He must be asleep," said Valerie.

They walked through the stable door into the kitchen. The portable tube went on chattering to itself from the all-steel draining board by the sink. Tom Jonty's wheelchair was facing it, but he was fast asleep. A newspaper, undoubtedly open at the Racing Page, had fallen across his knees.

"I thought so!" whispered Valerie, in order not to wake him.

"THEY'RE OFF!" shouted Jonty, at the top of his lungs.

Tom Jonty woke up at once, snuffling and clearing his throat. "What? " he said, startled. "What's that?... Oh, it's you, you daft get!"

Valerie laughed.

"And Val! Come in! Come in and sit down, gel!"

"We ARE in," said Jonty.

Valerie went across to the horsehair sofa and sat down plumb in the middle of it. The pleasure of sitting on it brought a little smile to her lips.

"Must have dozed off!" said Tom Jonty. "I've been wondering what had happened to you two. I mean you three," he added with a quick glance at Valerie.

Turning, he looked scornfully at the television announcer. "What's HE on about?" he asked, jerking a hand impatiently.

"He's warning the kids about frightening the dog-food out of the cats with their crackers, or the cat food out of the dogs with bangers, I'm not sure which."

"Turn him off!" said Tom Godley.

His son walked over the to the draining board to do as he was bidden. The kitchen was then completely in the dark. He found the light switch and clicked it on.

"That's better! What about a drink?" said Tom.

"Thought you'd never get round to it! In the fridge, isn't it?"

It was the size of a small anteroom, full of bottles. There was no room for anything else.

"Where do you keep your food, Dad?" asked Jonty, ironically.

"You're looking at it," said Tom Godley.

"I thought you'd got the booze under control?" asked the younger Godley, turning to look at him.

"I have! I only drink between meals."

"And for meals?" asked Valerie.

"I skip them! I'm on a diet!"

"Oh, that's not good, Mr Godley! You have to get your vitamins and trace elements, et cetera."

"Yes, you must listen to her, Dad! She studied nutrition as part of her course. Beer for you, Val?"

She nodded assent.

"I'm listening," said Tom Jonty.

Jonty took a bottle of Pale Ale across to Valerie.

"Where's the glass?" asked Valerie.

"Where'd you think?... In the sink," said Jonty.

"Don't use words that rhyme," said Valerie smugly.

"What?" asked Jonty, taken by surprise. "Oh, yes! Touché! You're right!" He smiled. "A smart little minx, aren't you?"

"That's one of the things you like about me, isn't it?... I'll do the glasses," she said, rising from the sofa.

"Who wants glasses?" asked Jonty.

"I do!" she said.

He knew he had been admonished.

"Well," said Godley Senior, "How're the printed books, son?"

"I'm working my notice!"

"I knew that wouldn't last!"

"It would have lasted if Sofia hadn't asked for a divorce and Valerie hadn't seduced me!"

"Well, I like that!" protested Valerie, turning round to stare at him.

"Would it?" asked Tom Godley, heavily.

"No!" said his son. "You're right! It couldn't, could it? The Country of the O'Grady's."

Valerie crossed from the sink to Tom Godley's chair. "Don't drink out of the bottle! Let me pour it for you," she said, taking Tom's beer out of his hand before he could protest.

She poured skilfully, and gave it back to him in the glass.

"There you are, Mr Godley!"

"Tom!" said Tom Godley, taking it.

"What?... Oh, all right! Tom," she said.

"That's better!" he said. And then, quickly: "Why don't you two come and live with ME?"

"Oh Christ! What – here?" asked Jonty, in consternation. "The Solihull Stockbroker Belt! I hear you even have to carry handkerchiefs to wipe your nose. Is that true?... I prefer to live in a house where you can grow mushrooms in the cupboards. I'm fond of mushrooms. Without soil, too... You can't do that, here, can you?"

"Never tried! What do you say, Val?"

"Why don't YOU come and live with US?" asked Valerie.

"Hey, that's a splendid idea!" said Jonty. "On your money, we could clean the place up a bit, and buy lots of liquid fertilizer for the mushrooms."

"And I might, at that!" asserted Godley Senior, with some enthusiasm. "So be careful what you say!... You'll be looking for another job, I suppose, Arnold, lad?"

"He says there aren't any jobs. Not for him!" put in Valerie quickly, looking fondly at Arnold. "He says he's a peg without a hole, not even a square one. But I don't believe that."

"No, it's true!" said Jonty, and took a large swallow of his beer. "What can I *do?* I ask you – what?"

"My goodness!" said Valerie. "The beer's making you morbid. That's not very complimentary to us, is it, Tom?"

"He'll be all right in a minute, Val!... I know what you mean, son. I didn't feel human myself until I started gambling for a living. Being human is being yourself. Being what you want to be, being what you CAN be... FINDING what you can be. There ain't much scope fer that, these days! You've got to be what they bleedin' want you to be, smartish!"

"That's it! ARNOLD JONTY WANTED. GOOD SALARY FOR RIGHT MAN. APPLY INCOGNITO." Jonty sucked in his cheeks, puckered his mouth, and let his eyeballs rise upward in his head. "Bloody hell!" he said.

"I s'pose Turf Accountancy suits me, because Life itself is one great big bloody gamble," said Tom, still musing on his last comment.

"But there must be a niche for Arnold, SOMEWHERE!" said Valerie, not without exasperation.

"Oh, yes, niches!" said Jonty. "There are niches everywhere... They're just not Jonty-shaped... Upall-shaped, Clatworthy-shaped, Dummock-shaped, even Newey-shaped, yes! But—"

Jonty looked across at Valerie, let his jaw hang, and trying to drop his lower eyelids to the level of his cheekbone, continued: "—There's only one niche I fit into."

"Don't be vulgar!" said Valerie.

"Being a gambler's being alive, see!" put in Tom, thinking aloud. "It's the way the Universe runs itself. See what I mean?"

"Who's Dummock?" asked Valerie.

"Oh, somebody I knew a long time ago, before Cambridge. God rest his soul!"

"Why – is he dead?"

"To everything that is 'not-Dummock' – yes!"

"Oh, one of THEM!" said Valerie.

"Don't worry! You can always work for me again, son."

"What would I do – make the tea and answer the telephone?... No, you have to be good at sums to do your job."

"Well!" said Valerie, with some asperity, "What CAN you do?"

"I can drink a lot of beer!" said Jonty, immediately. "I can compose notices, and pin them up in public places. I can make friends – with some people; and understand a few others. I know a good book from a bad book, and a good writer from a punk. I can swear pretty good. I can love you, and make you happy!... To name but a few... Then I've had it!... I don't believe in Salvation through the Common Market. Or Higher Production Figures. And I don't believe in handing the Reins of Power over – nor the values of Privilege and Class – to the Glorious Youth of the Country! So, in normal parlance, that adds up to bugger-all squared!"

Jonty held up his arms like a priest, and intoned: "In the Great Race of Life, I am Unplaced... Not even a helpless gambler like my Dad is going to put his money on an outsider like me! Hey, Pa?"

"Not so much of the helpless!" said Tom Godley. "There's a lot of us, you know!"

Jonty cocked his head to one side and listened.

"What's that?"

They all listened. Tom Jonty said: "Sounds like a fire engine! A long way off. Don't worry! It's on the wrong side of the river... How's the beer?"

"Marvellous!" said Jonty. Then sang: "Beer, Beer, Marvellous Beer," to a well-known tune. "Only it's finished," he said.

Valerie got up to fetch him some more.

Jonty's father took the opportunity to lean over the armrest of his chair and ask softly: "What the bloody hell DO you believe in, son?"

"Her!" said Jonty. "And what she's making!... Shhh!"

Valerie came back to give him his beer. Jonty took it, smiling.

She returned his smile, but did not speak; she simply moved her place to the other armchair, opposite to him. She sat leaning forward, her elbows on her knees; the weight inside her pried them a little apart; her fingertips covered her eyes, as if she was trying to concentrate on and assist the child in its arduous and solitary task of growing.

When he saw her like that, it touched, somewhere, something deeply tentative in him; and it aroused him, made him want her. But there was no chance of making love to Valerie, now.

He looked across at his father.

Tom Godley was in the middle of knocking the top off another bottle of beer on the armrest of his wheelchair. It came off cleanly, without a drop spilled. It took years of practice to do that.

But the child and its mother had had no time to practice; Jonty closed his eyes and prayed – to whom he did not know – that they would get it right first time, the two of them, and that the child would have five good senses and come whole into the world, although he felt deeply that the world did not deserve it. He opened his eyes and looked at Valerie.

She was still, still.

"What's wrong, Val?" he asked, in alarm.

"Nothing! I'm fine! He – she – was kicking. I wanted to feel it – and think about feeling it."

Her eyes were bright. Her long blonde hair was streaming down her face.

'Our delicate-looking gold stays delicate-looking gold!' thought Jonty, in irony.

"You didn't tell me!" he said aloud.

"There'll be other times," she said tenderly.

"I know! But you promised!" he answered, a little petulant, but mollified by the affection in her mood.

She'd got a lovely bit of *tessitura*, now. Does having a baby improve the female voice? It sounded more musical, with more harmonies.

Was it? Or had she had it all the time and he just hadn't noticed?

If not, why not? He should have oughted to notice a thing like that. JONTY'S PREGNANCY SERVICE FOR OPERA SINGERS. That sounded good. HAVE A JONTY BABY AND IMPROVE YOUR TESSITURA.

He'd probably be good at a thing like that. He'd certainly like doing it! Maybe he could earn a living at it?

MUSICAL INSEMINATION BY DONOR. M.I.D. Mmmm!... Might have possibilities...

'Am I getting drunk?... And what the hell am I going to do for a job?... I don't bloody know!'

He emptied his drink in one long throat-sweetening gurgle. 'So, for the moment, I'm going to have another beer.'

"Like some beer, anybody?" he asked, getting up.

Valerie shook her head.

"Just put it by my chair, son. I'll be through this one in a minute. Anyway," added Tom Godley, apropos of nothing anybody had recently said, "Gambling is fun. Besides, it makes you rich!"

"It makes *you* rich," said Valerie. "Not everybody."

"Yes, it makes me rich!" agreed Tom Godley.

'But afterwards. What about afterwards? I can't go on drinking beer for ever. Can I? Or can I? Is there such a thing as a professional beer-taster? Like a tea-taster. I know quite a lot about beer, really. Nearly as much as I know about frigidity in spinsters of both sexes. I should write a thesis: 'The Physical Ephects of Phrigidity on Belieph and

Phornication in Spinsters' by Arnold Jonty. Sounds all right.... Still, I'd rather taste beer for a living. Does Guinness employ only Irishmen?'

"Wouldn't it be nice if we had a bonfire?" asked Valerie, suddenly.

Jonty looked at her with admiration.

"Now, why didn't I think of that?" he asked, sarcastically.

"Because I thought of it, first," Valerie said, ingenuously.

"But that's no reason why I shouldn't have thought of it as well. You're only stating that you thought of it BEFORE I did. Whereas, what I'm trying to inquire into are the reasons WHY I didn't think of it first."

"You're getting drunk," said Valerie.

"That's funny! What I said sounded crystal clear to me... Anyway, I LIKE getting drunk and BEING drunk."

"I had a bonfire once," said Tom.

"There's nothing clever about that. Everybody has a bonfire once."

"Not like my bonfire!"

"What was special about your bonfire?" asked Jonty, not realizing where his father was going...

"Well, for one thing, it wasn't Bonfire Night! And for another – I was the Guy!"

Jonty looked at his father. Realization dropped like a cold stone inside him.

"Christ!" he said. "That! I thought that was an accident!"

17

Valerie was perplexed.

Something was happening between father and son that she didn't understand or like. Jonty was looking at his father with an expression of horror on his face, and Tom was looking back at him in sorrow.

"I know what you're thinking, son! But, no! I didn't... I didn't know you'd come in. Must have been fast asleep. I didn't hear a thing."

"And didn't you care?"

"I was tight as a newt. How the hell did I know you was upstairs?"

"But why?... What were you thinking of?"

"Son! It's hard to explain."

"Try! Why not try?"

His father took a deep breath.

"Your mother – after she went—." There was a catch in his voice. "D'you understand, son?"

Jonty understood very well.

He nodded. He knew how the emptiness had opened under his own feet, the void of no-feeling he carried around with him, the loneliness of her loss. His responses were different, that was all.

"I didn't want to go on. There was nothing for me. So I thought!"

"Yasus! And with Old Whatsit next door!"

"I know, son. It was terrible. I must have bin off my chump."

"What ARE you two talking about?" asked Valerie. "Is this a game? Do I have to stand on the side-lines, or what?"

They ignored her.

"Now," said Tom, "if it had been this house! What a blaze that would have been!"

"Now, stoppit! Stoppit, both of you!" said Valerie, who had by now put some of the pieces together, and was angered by their exclusion of her. "You've had a drink too much. Stoppit!"

Tipsily, Jonty began to laugh. "Hey! Is there any law that says a man can't set fire to his own house?"

"Why not? It's a free country!"

Valerie sat up straight in her chair.

"If you two think I'm going to let you set fire to this lovely big house, you're mistaken."

"Plenty more houses about!" said Tom, winking.

"But it's so spacious and lovely!"

"That's exactly why it should be burnt!" said Jonty, playing Devil's Advocate.

"NO! I WON'T LET YOU! NO!"

"All right! All right! It's all right, love!… Just speculating. The free mind! YOU know!"

"Yes, I know! I know exactly in what ways your mind speculates!" she said, sceptically. "But—?"

"Yes?"

"—We could have a Guy Fawkes of our own, couldn't we?"

"Of course, we could!" said Jonty, only too ready to pacify her.

"Good!" she said, as happy as a child, and as practical. "What can we use?"

"Have a look round," said Tom. "There should be a cupboard or two with a few old clothes knocking about, somewhere," he said vaguely.

"Right!" said Jonty, getting up. "Let's start upstairs."

Tom sat in his wheelchair, deep in his thoughts, slowly sipping his beer. Jonty held out his hand to Valerie, and they went out together, clasping hands.

As they searched, opening all the doors of the huge fitted wardrobes, moving from room to empty room, Jonty marvelled at how easily Valerie managed to carry the child inside her, a whole child, not merely a part of one: a foot, or a fist, but all of it, right down to the bed-wetting and nappy-filling and smiling-and-sucking bits, and without even seeming to notice!

She could bend and stoop and crouch without effort: it was extraordinary! She must be as roomy as one of these wardrobes, tucking away bits and pieces unexpectedly in odd corners.

And to think, the first time he'd spoken to her in that pub, he'd been convinced she hadn't even got space for a whole pint of beer! You just never could tell, could you?

To Jonty, it didn't seem beyond the bounds of possibility that the little bugger inside her might come out wearing a set of modish Carnaby Street diapers, with a full set of teeth and settled drinking habits, like his Dad – another headache for the clan of the O'Gradys!

"I think that'll do," said Valerie.

Jonty collected in his arms all that they had managed to glean, so he was almost hidden by a sizeable bundle when, led by Valerie, they went downstairs.

"What have you found?" asked Tom.

"Oh, lots of old rubbish!" said Jonty, dumping the stuff in a heap in the middle of the kitchen floor. "Now, where did I leave my beer?"

"Oh, look! There's enough to make several lovely Guys, here, isn't there, Tom? It'll be such fun!"

"I propose," said Jonty, holding his glass aloft, "that Our Guy should be a figure of composite bastardy."

"Come again?" queried Tom Jonty. "Cheers, anyway!" he added, holding his beer above his head, before taking a long hard pull at it.

"People we know! Isn't that what you mean?" said Valerie, in reply.

"Exactly! A bit of the General. A bit of The Pettigrew. A bit of Big Rev. *Und so weiter.* But one Guy – with a bit from each."

"Fine!" said Tom, swallowing his beer, lustily and noisily. "Your enemies are my enemies, son! Bring 'em any time... It's Liberty Hall here – Uncle's!... We'll shear 'em like sheep."

"But I fancy making a Guy for each of them," said Valerie. "One for the General. One for the Pettigrew. You know! They're such lovely subjects... Anyway, look at the stuff we've got! Why waste it?" asked Valerie, with a gesture that swept all the materials together into it.

"Okay! You've persuaded me!"

Jonty put down his beer and looked about him.

"Let's compromise! First the composite, and then the others."

"All right! Let's begin!" said Valerie.

"This jacket will do for a start," he said, making a run at the pile. "If we can stuff it with something shapeless, and huge, we'll have the Clatworthy bosom to a tee!"

"Spelling's shaky, son! There's no tee in 'bosom'."

"The way I spell it, there is!"

"What about these two cushions – like this?" asked Valerie. "They look about right."

"That's it!... Marvellous!... And if I tie this tissue – there! – like that... 'Folks, this is one of those magic moments.' A delicate ribbon nestling in your cleavage brings back Romantic Memories!"

"Fool!" giggled Valerie. "Who's next?"

"Maybe a bit of The Pettigrew... And let's keep the party clean, folks!"

"Her face!" squealed Valerie, with glee.

"That's going to be difficult."

"Why?"

"I've never come across anything to match that complexion... Unless it's a bit of badly-knitted beige wool!"

"I know what we can use. The dishcloth!" said Valerie, holding it triumphantly in the air and shaking it to emphasise her discovery.

"Perfect match! Clever girl... But how're we going to fake those bristles of hers?"

"String?" asked Tom. "There's plenty o' that."

"Near enough! There! Now – two large owl-eyes... Lovely!"

He added the two lids of empty cocoa tins that he had discovered on a shelf under the sink, and stood back to assess the effect.

"How's that?" he asked. "Jonty Cosmetics Incorporated Originates the Infinite Face!' But maybe three eyes would be better – symbolic – truer to her character?"

"Christ!" said Tom. "If I worked with people who looked like that, I'd – I'd—" At a loss for words, he faded.

"You'd what?" asked Jonty.

"I dunno!" said his father, lamely, and swallowed a lot of beer. "But I'd do summat," he added, wiping the froth from his lips on an old scarf he picked off the heap.

"Well, we *are* doing something, aren't we?" said Jonty.

"On with the good work... What about the well-known Heffler nose?"

"What are we going to use for THAT?" asked Valerie.

"And the well-known Heffler fingers for picking the aforesaid Heffler nose?"

"Oh, horrible!" said Valerie. "Don't be horrible!"

"There's a pound of beef sausage in the fridge, if that's any good," put in Tom.

"Just the thing! Close replicas of the Heffler digits!"

And, as an afterthought, Jonty said, musingly: "Uncooked, I hope!"

He went over to the fridge and opened it; after gazing into it for some time, and then searching behind the bottles, he asked:

"Where? There's nothing but beer in here."

"Look in the freezer!" said Tom Jonty.

Jonty did so.

"Here they are! But I'm going to have to put his fingers under the tap. They're frozen together."

"And his nose," said Valerie.

"Here you are!" said Jonty. "Wipe off the dewdrop first."

Valerie took it and attempted to place it on the half-formed composite visage.

"This nose is insubordinate!" said Valerie. "It won't stay in place."

"Use string! Tie it on!... That's it. Lovely!... 'Now the House of Jonty Brings You the Ultimate Face – With a Light, Fresh, Fragrant, Oven-Ready Conk!'... Ta-ra!... We're short on fingers."

"Put one hand in its pocket," suggested Valerie.

"Atta girl!" said Jonty. "With a long thumb sticking out."

"I'm looking for the Upall legs!" said Val.

"Minmm!... Sexy!... Why Upall? Upall's all right."

"I don't think so! He's only out for what he can get and you can go hang!... Anyway, his legs don't bend in the middle when he walks."

"Physiologically impossible! But I guess you're right about—. Why not stuff his trousers with *The Times*? That's pretty stiff stuff!... Got any old copies of *The Times*, Pop?"

"No! Don't read it! Racing column's no good. Only *Daily Expresses*."

"Nearly as stiff! That'll do," said Jonty.

"What about its hair?" asked Val.

"No hair!" said Tom Jonty, emphatically, looking about him.

Jonty went across to the effigy with an item of his father's toiletry from the sill behind the sink.

Valerie's remark about Upall had set up vague and uneasy vibrations in his memory that he couldn't quite place at the moment.

"Why not give it a squeeze or two of toothpaste?"

He executed a couple of deft strokes with the tube.

"Like that!"

He straightened.

"Not bad!" said Valerie.

Jonty stepped back a pace and admired his handiwork.

"Cream Makes Simple Things Super!" he intoned. "Of course, you've got to remember – it's all in the mind! The prisoners in the dock don't look exactly like their originals. But the intention's there!... I've been thinking that maybe—"

Valerie waited.

"Yes?" she said, questioningly.

"Oh, it doesn't matter!" he said, impatient with himself.

"Yes, it does," she said firmly. "Tell me!"

"Well – I was wondering if Crehan's effigy shouldn't be here. He's probably the biggest figure of bastardy of all, if the truth be told," he said musingly.

"Who's Crehan?" asked Valerie.

"Never considered him in that light before."

He was lost for a moment, wondering at himself. Then, recollecting Valerie's question, he answered vaguely:

"....Oh, Crehan!... Somebody I knew a few years ago."

"All right, don't tell me!" said Valerie sharply. "I can bear not to know."

"A friend of Sofia's...." he added quickly. "No! I'll just imagine he's there. I'll burn him in my mind!"

"You'll get soot on the brain, son," said Tom.

Jonty started gathering more of the scattered articles together, rather feverishly.

"Now, I'll make a real Heffler," he said.

"And I'm going to make a real Upall," said Valerie.

In silence, they worked steadily at the guy-making.

As they took shape, Tom Jonty said: "Better use one of them old armchairs to burn them in."

"But—" said Valerie, her attention diverted.

"—No buts!" said her father-in-law, taking his chance. "They've had their day."

"But they're nearly new!" objected Valerie.

"Yes! This is their day!" said Tom.

"You're terrible!" said Valerie, laughing.

Jonty, unusually silent, was already busy arranging the victims in one of the armchairs.

"Let's push it outside," he said, moving towards the conservatory, with less than his usual co-ordination.

"Not that way!" said Tom. "It won't go through the glass-house door. You'll have to take it through the hall."

With an exaggerated flourish, Jonty swung the armchair on its castors, like a Bumping Car at a fair, and steered it inaccurately towards the kitchen-door and into the hall. Once there, it moved easily on the large tiles; but the castors screeched in the emptiness, rebounding from wall to wall.

Valerie covered her ears.

"Ow!... Worse than chalk on a blackboard," she said.

Tom came through the open doorway in his wheelchair at a rate of knots after them. He had clamped a fresh bottle of beer between his knees.

Jonty, affected by the excitement and beginning to show signs that he had already had one too many, rushed by him, going back into the kitchen again.

"Matches! Matches!" he called.

He returned a moment later, flourishing a large white plastic container of paraffin, as well as the matches.

"Thought the three ghoulsh might be thirshty," he said. "Thirsty!" he repeated correctly, to show that he was still in control of his tongue and the situation.

He unscrewed the plastic top from the container and upended it over the chair and the three Guys lolling preposterously in it. The paraffin soaked into the effigies and began to run down the leather and glisten darkly on the floor.

Oblivious, Jonty still went on pouring. Small rivulets began to snake their way towards the walls, and settle against the high wooden wainscots.

"That's enough!" said Valerie. "You're making an awful mess in the hall."

"Don't worry! It could do with a clean," said Tom Jonty, taking a pull at his bottle.

"But I do worry! Mess offends me!"

"Yes! Don't forget she's a profeshal," said Jonty, losing a consonant in the articulation. "She's a professional," he repeated deliberately, correcting himself. "Right! Open the door."

Valerie pulled open the heavy oaken door and wedged it with the articulating rubber mat from the porch. The night sky, made a little vague and hazy by the smoke of bonfires, was nevertheless fine and clear and sprinkled with stars. It had been raining and the lawns were sodden. A slight tinge of orange seemed to suffuse the night; and the trees, bare of leaves, stood out like half-imagined skeletons. Except for a few shouts diluted from a long way off, and the sound of the wind through the skeletal limbs, everywhere was quiet.

She faced into the streaming air and breathed deeply; it delighted her to fill her lungs like that and feel its movement through her long tresses. With a slight sense of reluctance, she went back into the house and along the hallway to Jonty, who was swaying slightly on his feet and fumbling with a box of matches.

"Arnold! Not in here! You'll—"

Jonty struck a match and threw it laughingly into the air and watched it arcing towards the Guys.

"—Arnold, stop fooling!"

As it landed, unexpectedly still alight, a great whooshing flame blasted upwards with a noise like a train rushing into a tunnel. Jonty staggered back with the surprise and shock of it. Valerie screamed and put her hand to her mouth.

"Christ!" cried Tom. "What the hell did you do that for, Jonty?"

He wheeled himself as near as he could get to the conflagration and threw out the remainder of his beer over it; but it made no difference.

Jonty coughed and spluttered, rubbing his singed moustache and eyebrows.

A blanket of dark smoke began to fold and unfold itself under the ceiling, opening itself out into the hallway, like someone covering a bed.

"Arnold! Do something!" screeched Valerie.

Tom Jonty propelled himself rapidly back into the kitchen and returned a moment later, holding a broom in front of his chair, like a huge feeler.

"Here! Push it out with this. Hard! Fast!"

Hazily, Jonty took it from his father and thrust at the blazing chair.

Unfortunately, the castors were wrongly set, and it shot to the side of the open door, obliquely, into a corner of the hall. It bumped into a wall, rebounded, and began to flare up more fiercely than ever. Jonty stood staring at the burning chair with its quartet of fiery effigies, as if mesmerised.

"What are we going to do?" cried Valerie. "We'll all be on fire at this rate!"

"Pull it out!" shouted Tom. "With the broom! Pull it out!"

Jonty didn't move. Fumes of smoke were mingling behind his eyes with the fumes of alcohol.

Desperately, Valerie made a dart and snatched the broom from his hands and ran to the burning armchair. She hooked it over an arm of the chair, and began to pull. The chair swivelled slightly, but did not give.

"Help her!" shouted Tom.

Valerie pulled again, hard, and the chair started to follow the line of the broom handle. The effigies were burning fiercely now. She moved slowly backwards, towards the open door.

"Help her, you idiot!" shouted his father again.

Before he had managed to get himself into gear, Jonty saw Valerie stop, hold herself stiff for a moment, and then bend slowly forward, clutching her stomach. She gave a low moaning groan and half turned towards him.

Even through the fumes in his head, and in the smoky light of the flames, he could see that her face had gone very white.

"Val" he called, desolate.

She turned fully round, as if in response to his call, and took a step towards him; then she began to crumple slowly, falling to the floor, and drawing up her knees as she lay there.

Like a man who had been frozen in ice and was now thawing out, imperfectly, Jonty started to move; but before he could reach Valerie, Tom had whipped in, as if discharged down a shoot, stopping just short of her.

She was groaning.

"Get hold of her, lad!"

Jonty grasped her clumsily under the arms and started to drag her away from the region of the burning chair. But she resisted, struggled to her feet and, standing weakly against him, leaned her head on his chest, breathing heavily.

In the excitement, pushing on the arms, Tom Jonty's adrenalin had forced him out of the wheelchair, and he was now standing upright by her, both feet on the ground.

"Come on, gel! How're you feeling?"

She looked up at Tom, breathlessly, with an expression of puzzlement, her blonde hair mussed about her white vulnerable face.

Seeing her thus, a surge of shame passed over Jonty, strong and cold as a wave of the Northern seas, sobering him.

"Are you all right, love?" he asked, hesitantly.

"Yes, I think so! The worst of it has passed. But it's coming. I know it is! Ooh!"

She gasped again.

"What is it? What is it?"

Jonty's eyes were fixed on her, as if he would never stop looking.

"I don't know! A funny sharp feeling. Inside. Low down... I think you'll have to get me to hospital, soon... What about the Guys?"

Jonty watched her with an intensity of seeing, mixed with pain and humiliation, that was new to him, so that he did not even hear her question.

Tom threw a glance over his shoulder at the glowing chair and its burden.

"Leave it where it is! Can't do any harm! It should burn itself out," he said.

Valerie's expression of puzzlement was turning to wonder. With a slight movement of one hand towards Jonty, she said, in a vibrant whisper:

"Look at your Dad!"

The urgency in her voice made him turn from her, to do as he was told. He looked at his father.

Tom was standing by his chair, on his own two feet.

"Yasus!" said Jonty, in amazement. "He's standing up!... Dad, you're standing up!... What the—? That bloody doctor said—!"

"Never mind that, now! I thought she'd had it!... Don't hang around. Go and get her a bloody ambulance!"

When Jonty still stood gazing at him, he barked: "NOW, son!"

As Tom spoke, he stepped backwards, feeling for the arms of the invalid chair with his hands and, finding them, lowered himself weakly into it.

Held at the centre of his own whirling emotions and astonished into silence, his son watched him without moving.

Valerie's face showed her wonder still; but in her eyes was a strange brightness, a kind of triumph, as she looked at Jonty's father, suddenly weary, sitting there, in the middle of the vast empty hall, the unrecognisable remains of the Guys smouldering in the charred frame of the chair, their acrid smoke emptying, unravelling out of the open door into the night, like the last skeins of an immense grief, now nearly gathered and winnowed, drifting, drifting away into the night...

He lifted his head, slow, unseeing, like an animal that has just slaked its thirst, and said, quietly, gently: "Get the hell out of here!... Valerie – you go and sit in the kitchen!... Go! Do as I tell you!"

She hesitated and looked in befuddlement at Jonty, who nodded assent.

"Better still," said Tom Jonty, "lie on the couch till the ambulance comes."

His arm round her shoulders, Jonty walked her into the kitchen, sat her down, leaned her back, picked up her legs and, with great tenderness, placed them on the leather sofa.

That done, he suddenly knelt down on the floor, beside the couch. "Are you all right?" he was asking her, in a small voice.

She could hear a new pain in it.

"Yes," she said, lovingly.

She smiled at him.

"Fine!... I'm all right."

"Truly?"

"Truly."

Jonty bowed his head and leaned it gently against her thigh.

"Val?" he said.

"Yes?"

"I'm sorry!"

His entire posture was full of contrition. She reached out and stroked his thick curly hair.

"I know," she said.

And, as if she was comforting a child:

"There, it's all right, now... There... there!"

"I'm sorry!... I feel so ashamed of myself!"

"It's all right! Really!... You'd better go now. Do as your father says. Phone for an ambulance."

"Should I?"

"Yes!" she said firmly, with a small giggle, pushing him to his feet.

"All right," he said, submissively.

Jonty got up and walked like a man in a dream to his father's office. He ordered the ambulance and sat down to wait. Only, there was a seething restlessness inside him that would not let him be. He got to his feet and paced up and down; but it was not enough. He needed space. He needed to be alone. He needed time. He needed to know what he was feeling and what he was thinking.

He ran out into the large hall, empty except for the figure of his father, alone, in the invalid chair, and the remains of their abortive bonfire smouldering near one of the corners. He ran past his father, and the glowing and growing ash, and out into the night.

He needed the balm of the darkness upon him.

18

Three weeks later, Jonty was walking along the High Street, Colchester, looking for the kind of shop Valerie had described to him, and re-assessing the tricks of fate that had brought him to where he was at the moment, when he discovered, yet again, that he was still immensely tickled and surprised by it all; but, at the same time, never having pictured himself as a father like his father before him, he was far from sure that he was going unreservedly to like it.

The future seemed even fuller of disturbing questions than usual.

For example, as time passed, and as he eased himself into fatherhood, would he grow to be more like his own parent, or less so? Would his father, translated forcibly into grandfatherhood, grow more like his own son, or less so? Or more and more like himself?

Questions like that were far from easy to answer, and future prospects in that direction, if contemplated deeply, could be disquieting.

But the main question he was trying to sort out was: How does it actually feel, here and now, to be a father?

The odd thing was that his present feelings seemed to be made up, predominantly, of the same kind of material they had been made up of when he wasn't a father.

Was that normal?

True, there seemed to be a few extras thrown in: "It's not mine! No chin, and a nose like a toothpick."

And, at first: "My God! look at that bit! It's like a small dried apricot – all wrinkled and brick-coloured. I know she's a girl, but is it all right?"

And: "Thank heavens, the poor little bugger can't actually see what the Matron looks like. It would want to go back where it came from!"

And later: "Was that a smile?... It was a smile, wasn't it? I think the little darling knows me!"

And: "I've never seen you so happy, Val! Your eyes are so bright and your skin has the bloom of a ripe peach. Sorry for the cliché!... Just what have we done, girl?... What have we bloody done?"

And he kissed her.

On Bonfire Night, the small Cottage Hospital near his father's house had been full; so that Valerie had had to be taken to the Maternity Ward of the huge Queen Elizabeth Hospital at Selly Oak, near the University. An hour or so later, she had given birth to a daughter, several weeks premature.

It had been an easy birth – "Like shelling a pea!" the sister had said – and Valerie was fine. There had been no complications; the baby had been born with five good senses and, after a short initial period in an incubator, had continued to grow normally.

Most of which had made Jonty feel grateful to the natural forces that during her pregnancy had been responsible for it all, and which he could only dimly wonder at.

But the shock of seeing the baby for the first time had been quite severe, and had not diminished for some days.

Nine months work for that!

Seeing it there, swaddled in its little flannelette cerements, had made him seriously question whether the baby-business was all that people cracked it up to be. If he'd have been the C.O. in charge of operations, he'd have had to take issue with those incomprehensible forces he'd mentioned a moment ago, and have had to try to handle things a bit differently.

For a start, he wouldn't have allowed that little beak of a nose to assert itself; and he would have had it dyed a better colour.

And those ears! Tiny as they were, they didn't augur well for the future.

Furthermore, that crying mechanism, which had unaccountably operated at full volume from Day One, would have had a neatly concealed on-off switch installed somewhere, for the convenience of Dad; and Mother should have been able to put the entire feeding process on some kind of automatic pilot... Not to mention the general muck-up at the blunt end. The less said about that the better!... In certain respects, it looked a pretty bleak prospect for some considerable time to come.

'Ah, well!' sighed Jonty. 'The Ugly Duckling's father and mother hadn't been any better off at the start of things, had they? And look what happened to them?... But who wants off-spring with feathers, a long sinewy neck, and webbed feet?'

At that moment, nearly at the end of the High Street, Jonty caught sidelong a flash of underwear from a window, and turned sharply into the doorway of the shop.

Before he knew it, he was halfway to a very tiny hardboard counter painted in garish stripes, under lights directed at varied angles out of small black tubes and so bright that they hurt his eyes.

He divined, at the same instant, he had come to the wrong place.

His eardrums were assaulted by very loud musical-type-noises, coming out of a loudspeaker at a volume that made it impossible to hear any actual music. Jonty reckoned it was at a decibel level that would soon induce deafness in the upper reaches of his listening equipment unless he could soon escape it; and it was undoubtedly being produced by one of those groups that had names like The Tin Airship or The Brass Monkeys.

But wasn't it too late to turn back and disappear out of the door?

Could he ignore that collection of assorted personages near the counter, and walk out? Were they sales assistants or customers?

When they saw Jonty hesitate, they all shrugged their shoulders and, with entirely expressionless faces, turned away, to a man – or was it, to a woman?

As he hesitated, one of them came out of a cubicle slightly larger than a matchbox, dressed in a midi-skirt that was herring-boned in wide bands of a luminous mauve colour. Above this a multi-coloured blouse was being worn; it still had a ticket on saying, authoritatively, SWISS VOILE.

But, surprisingly, below the midi-skirt, a pair of canary yellow bell-bottomed trousers protruded, made out of some kind of velveteen material.

The whole ensemble was adorning a body that gave the strong impression of having been machine-pressed, like a plastic coat-hanger: there wasn't a bump or projection in evidence from the top to the bottom of the figure.

Jonty stared: it stood to reason, there had to be a bump or two somewhere.

But where?

While he was thus occupied, the hermaphrodite stepped out of its midi-skirt, and twirled round and round in the bell-bottom trousers. There was a blinding flash of yellow, like a blast from a shotgun, and, in the middle of it, an androgynous smile.

Jonty turned away, rubbing his eyes, as if removing little balls of yellow shot from their corners, and went to the counter.

While he waited, the assorted personages were watching the hermaphrodite. They registered various shades of tiredness, boredom, indifference, derision and scorn – in turn, and all at the same time.

Eventually, one of the girls (who could have been one of the boys), with waist-length hair and a flour-coloured face, wandered, splay-footed, across to the counter, stood about a yard from Jonty, and waited.

Jonty also waited.

During the lull he noticed that, on this one, there was a bump or two – well concealed, it was true, but nevertheless there. Yes, this one was unmistakeably female.

He could tell... couldn't he?...

Suddenly, the girl jerked up her chin, rather vigorously and impatiently.

Jonty was being invited to state his business; he assumed that it was the particular version of 'the- customer-is-always-right' approach they currently favoured in this establishment.

"My wife," he began, "has asked me to get her a—"

He stopped.

The girl's face had put on a screwed-up look of pain and disbelief, as if he had started to talk to her in a heavy dialect of Canton Chinese.

"What? What you say?" she yelled.

Of course! He should have remembered!

The Brass Monkeys! He had somehow managed to filter them out of his auditory field.

Jonty, filling his lungs ready to begin again, suddenly changed his mind.

There were easier ways!

So he let his breath leak out, leaned towards the girl, and, in a normal voice, spoke into her ear.

She started back as if he had tried to spit down her eustachian tubes, and her lidded eyes opened wide.

Then, she shrugged her shoulders for the third or fourth time, turned, and slouched across to the group, where she appeared to communicate with the shoulder of one of them.

At the instant the message was completed, the recipient froze; then unfroze, and went quickly through a curtain at the rear of the little shop.

Jonty waited impatiently.

The messenger returned almost at once, accompanied by a huge man who, except for his complexion, had for some years been modelling himself on press photographs of Sonny Liston in his most menacing poses.

Jonty's impatience evaporated, to be replaced by another emotion he didn't have time to analyze before registering that the tiny, almost invisible moustache beneath the man's pugilistic nose did practically nothing to allay the purity of the aggression on his face. His fingers were the size of the thick frozen sausages they had hung on their Guy Fawkes, and – had he contracted a severe form of Derbyshire neck; or was it, really, solid muscle?

The man towered in front of Jonty like several storeys of Aberdeen granite; and Jonty was feeling as he had on many occasions in the past when he had hugged the walls of a public building for shade on a hot day: he sensed the little trickles of sweat following the furrow of his spine.

Suddenly, the man put his huge fists on the spot where his hips should have been and, over the unmusical typhoon coming out of The Brass Monkeys, bawled: "Listen, Mick! We don't want your sort here. Now, clear! Or I'll twist your bleeding head orf! See?"

Jonty was flabbergasted.

The man had a high falsetto voice.

"What's up? I only wanted a—"

"—Bugger orf!" came the piercing command.

"—feeding bra!"

"Get!" screeched the man, leaning forward over the frail counter and putting his two enormous fists on it.

Jonty got.

Outside, Jonty inhaled deeply, and caught sight of the shop-sign, jutting out at right angles to the door, which he hadn't seen on his way in.

It announced, in fussy white lettering: TINY'S BOUTIQUE. The signwriter would have painted it with heavy irony, surely?

Nothing to do with the Tiny Tot's business would ever be sold there, and Jonty felt very strongly that what Tiny had, Tiny could keep.

Toute la boutique!

Tiny had, in all probability, graduated from the BOUCHERIE business to the BOUTIQUE business; in which case, he would still have his cleavers hanging up on little nails behind his shop. No wonder his hands were full of frozen British sausages!

In this case, discretion clearly had been the better part of valour. Jonty was in no doubt that, had he demurred longer, he could now have been hanging in a refrigerated vault somewhere, with meat-hooks through his collar, waiting for Tiny's next mincing session.

Jonty decided, there and then, to walk back along the whole length of the street, looking for something very old-fashioned and very safe.

No, they wouldn't catch him a second time like that! Not if he could help it. Or even, not like that! They weren't going to catch him at all.

He came to a wide window – he had missed it on his way down the street – which had a lot of female garments in it spread out without any concern for the slightest aesthetic effect.

Whatsoever!

That seemed more promising! Although there were differences, it was certainly more like the kind of shop Valerie had described to him.

For instance, there was no lack of room, but this owner seemed to want to display as many items as possible in as small a space as possible.

Well, why not?

Jonty looked round for a sign.

There was no twee little board sticking out at right angles from the wall, as at Tiny's, that could easily be missed: the name was written in large clear letters above the lintel of the door, and across the frontage, as any self-respecting name should be.

It said: N. JOHNSON & CO. LINGERIE, DRAPERY. LADIES OUFITTERS.

That was more like it!

Mr Johnson clearly meant business. No 'Bugger orf' would be forthcoming from a man like him!

Jonty walked confidently into the shop.

It had a long deep interior, gloomy and quiet. Two substantial brown wooden counters, one to his right, and one to his left let themselves down from the light at the door into the dim depths at the bottom.

There were no customers; only a small bespectacled man standing behind the right hand counter, about halfway down, putting items of underwear into a small garment drawer.

Jonty walked across to him.

Could this be the owner?

The way he stood gave Jonty the impression that he had got knock-knees, and had always been bullied at school when he made mistakes on the rugger field.

Jonty felt an instant sympathy with him.

"Are you Mr N. Johnson & Company?" asked Jonty.

"I am that! What can I do for you?" whispered the man; and smiled broadly at Jonty.

When Jonty registered surprise, the man tapped his throat with a forefinger.

Jonty nodded in sympathy. He heard someone enter the shop behind him. Mr Johnson acknowledged the new customer with a brief nod that conveyed the message that he would be in attendance soon.

"I want a feeding bra, please," said Jonty, in a loud clear voice.

Mr Johnson's eyes flickered involuntarily as far as Jonty's pectorals before he recovered himself, leaned confidently across the counter, and whispered to Jonty that Sir hadn't quite meant what he had said, had he?

What Sir meant was—"

The next few words were almost inaudible; but before they disappeared forever among the sliding shelves of draperies, Jonty had managed to detain them just long enough to catch: "a nursing brassiere, Sir!" –like a whisper on tiptoe.

"Oh, do I?" asked Jonty loudly. "Yes, that's it. A nursing bra!"

N. Johnson & Company snapped to attention. Glancing right and then left very quickly, his myopic eyes glinted behind his spectacles.

'What's he looking at? Is he practising the Road Safety code?'

Then, quick as a flash from his own spectacle lenses, he turned round and abstracted one of the sliding boxes from the piled ranks of them above him. In the same smooth movement, he lowered and laid it on the counter in front of Jonty, and leaned towards him again.

"We shall have to find out..."

Mr Johnson's voice was getting quieter and quieter. By the time this utterance was over, which was very soon, he seemed to be whispering from inside a soundproof room.

Jonty had to guess what he had said. He guessed it was: "We shall have to find out the size!"

'Not so much of the we! How'd you propose to do that? I'm not having you wield your tape-measure round Valerie's whatsits!'

Mr Johnson was regarding Jonty steadily.

Then Jonty remembered what Valerie had told him:

'Thirty-four, B-cup. Inches, not centimetres!'

"Oh, yes!" said Jonty. "It's a thirty-four. B-cup."

"That's probably a 92 centimetres size?" whispered Mr Johnson, barely audible.

"What?" bellowed Jonty, baffled and anti-conspiratorial.

The woman who had come into the shop behind Jonty was now leaning on the counter a little below them, entranced by their performance. The volume of Jonty's voice brought pain to Mr Johnson's eyes and he jerked his head back with a snap. Mr Johnson looked conciliatingly at her. She smiled, and, with another snap, Mr Johnson bent himself down and began fiddling beneath the counter.

'Oh, so he really does work on elastic?'

Jonty began wondering if he had remembered the size correctly. Mr Johnson's figure of 92 had confused him. He had no wish to go through it all again, working out the metric.

'That's a thought!' he thought. 'Metricating the size of boobs, in A,B,C and D-cups. Plenty of overtime in that!... How far through the alphabet do they go, anyway?... It must be quite an experience coming up against a hundred-and-twenty "X" cup... Centimetres, that is!... Well into the Clatworthy class!'

Before Jonty was properly aware of what was going on, there was a rustle of brown paper and a blur of regulation pink, and Mr Johnson had snapped upright again and was handing him a neat little packet, with an expression on his face that said: "Here! Put it out of sight. That'll cost you three smackers!"

But what Mr Johnson's voice actually whispered was:

"That will be one pound and twenty-five new pence, please, Sir!... We sell them a little more cheaply than our rivals. They charge one pound and thirty new pence."

The last two sentences were uttered slightly more loudly than the first, in a kind of hoarse whisper, as though Mr Johnson had a heavy cold coming on.

Jonty asked: "Is it the sort that has hooks down the front to—?"

"—Yes, sir!"

His mouth shaped the words soundlessly and hurriedly, not allowing Jonty to complete his question, and Mr Johnson's expression was full of pain and disillusion.

His incredible embarrassment throughout the entire transaction was beginning to have its effect on Jonty: he began to feel a vague hysteria rising up in him.

That must have been why, in a voice which surprised even himself, and giving an impression of somebody trying to shatter a wine-glass in a two-minute silence round the cenotaph on Poppy Day, he trilled:

"Can I see it?"

The result could not have been worse if he had suddenly demanded that N. Johnson & Company take down its trousers.

It was plain that pure and absolute consternation ran like fire through the little man's veins, setting up a burning and enfeebling sensation in his knock-knees.

Jonty could have sworn that Mr Johnson was abbreviating himself before his very eyes, before he recovered and grasped the counter with an air of desperation, putting a stop to the process.

Jonty began to feel sorry for him, which, luckily, overcame the vague hysteria he had sensed in himself a moment ago.

Slowly, very very slowly, slow as the hour hand on his wristwatch, the little man began to undo a tiny corner of the packet.

In due course, shielding it from the lady some way down the counter with the palm of his hand, like a French tout selling dirty postcards in front of the Eiffel Tower, he showed Jonty a small square of cross-sewn pink material, while, as if he had nothing to do with what was going on, he looked the other way, smiling.

Jonty tried to get hold of it, but his fingers slipped on the cellophane wrapper inside the packet.

By persistence, he managed to pull the brassiere half out of its brown paper wrapping, but couldn't remove it entirely because Mr Johnson was leaning heavily on the other half of it.

When Jonty realized what Mr Johnson was doing, he gave up.

"Yes, all right! That'll do, I suppose," he sighed.

Mr Johnson moved with immense rapidity, as if still on elastic. Almost before Jonty had made his reply, he was offering the packet back to him, neatly re-wrapped.

"One twenty five pee," he mouthed, soundlessly.

"Yes. I know."

Jonty shaped the words silently, in return. Mr Johnson smiled broadly, feeling he had won.

Jonty reached into his pocket for the money and put the exact amount on the counter. Jonty was halfway out of the shop with his purchase, when he heard a pure-toned soprano saying loudly behind him:

"You'll be all right with that, sir! We sell quite a lot of them. You can always—"

Startled, Jonty turned round to look at the woman leaning on the counter. She had her back to him and was holding up a child's jersey to the light and examining it carefully.

'That's odd!'

Jonty looked away and regarded Mr Johnson instead. He was smiling happily at Jonty.

"Thank you, sir!" he said, in his normal voice.

It was a pure-toned soprano. No wonder he had wanted to keep on whispering!

Jonty hurried out.

What a morning!

First, Tiny, and now Mr Johnson!

What's up with the place?

Had the Town Council worked up a campaign for attracting counter-tenors and eunuchs to the Municipal Choir and were these two of the aspirants?

Or was it something in the drinking water?

Better watch it! He'd take no risks and drink beer with his meals, in future...

Anyway, what the hell was wrong with asking for a feeding bra?

He hadn't wanted it for himself. Had he looked as though he did?

If he'd demanded that Tiny or Mr Johnson produce a fishin' bra, or a huntin' bra, or a drinkin' bra, or even a shootin' bra, he could have better understood their reactions. But all he had needed was a common-or-garden nursing bra!

That kind of behaviour just gave you a pain in the tit, didn't it?...

He only hoped it would fit Valerie properly when he got it home, and she didn't find it too tight across the knees or baggy round the ankles and it didn't end up giving her a pain where it shouldn't.

He'd absolutely hate to be made to take it back, and have to stand through another performance of the swan-voiced and elastic-driven Mr Johnson.

Oh, yes! Once was much too much, wasn't it?

19

L ife was good!

While he worked out his notice as Lecturer (Probationary) in English, Jonty was spending as little time as he decently could at St Anne's.

For the present, he was at home.

He had been occupied for most of the morning in the cellar of Bennet's Folly, cleaning, emery-clothing and Painting his Victorian baby-cot – he still had to remember to ask the landlord whether or not he could borrow it.

As he worked, he found his mind turning over, yet again, the topsoil of recent events, and musing on where he was at, and how things had changed, and how he hoped he had grown more able to learn from, and cope with, life as he encountered it in its multifarious tropes and figures of bastardy.

If he had, it was due mainly to Valerie, and her impact on him. Of that much he was certain!...

He raked over and over his experiences and their meanings, putting a fine tilth on them. It was an exercise as necessary as breathing to Jonty. Only then – sparse though they may be – could his little seeds of wisdom grow.

Whether they would grow was another matter!

That depended on the supply of nutrients: particularly, the creative and comic scepticism of his mind, the humanistic tenor of his convictions, his tendency to prefer truth to falsity, his deeply vivifying relationship with Valerie, now the coming of the child, and perhaps, most of all, luck.

He still didn't know what to make of all the feelings he had had about The Bairn; but he was aware of something – he couldn't define what – rising inside him like water in a lock, a kind of quintessential excitement, a vital fluid, which suffused his veins and capillaries and which was at the same time a wonderful balm to his spirit.

No matter what he thought he felt, or thought he would like to feel, or thought he ought to feel, that is how he actually felt: alive.

It made him feel alive up to the hilt of his being.

Of course, he felt, as usual, beset by quandaries.

For instance, now that Jonty Senior was living with them, were they going to stay at Bennet's Folly, or move to a new base?

Maybe, until Valerie was properly on her feet and until The Bairn had reached the apex of the merde output-graph, it would be better to remain where they were?

He didn't know.

'Dear Mother,' he began in his head, *'What do you think? Do we stay or move?*

'But leave that one for the minute!

'It's been a long time since I wrote to you. And the big news of the times is that Valerie has had a baby girl. I'm hoping it – Sorry! – she will grow up like her mother and her grandmother, not like her dad and grandad. So far, we don't know what to call her. I've named her The Bairn, in lieu of. She is very wee, but already herself. I mean, I want her to have your wisdom and kindness and intelligence. And Val's methodicalness and peace and sensibility. You know! And when we get married, we are going to invite her to her mother and father's

wedding; and, later on, she can invite us to her Christening. Then we shall know what her name is. It all depends when the divorce from Sofia comes through, but I don't see any snags there. We've given her all the evidence she needs. And what a piece of evidence she is! Such a tiny phenomenon!

'*Dad is on his feet again! Would you believe it? Metaphorically and physically! In between studying those Blue Form Books he loves so much, and shouting lots of names and numbers and odds into the blower he's had installed here, he's practising his ability to walk again. He says he's losing weight. If he is, he isn't losing bulk. Like Mr Pyecraft, in that H.G. Wells story you read me once. He's got a few people running a little office in Colchester now, as well as the big one in Brum. Pyecraft turned into a balloon and floated up to the ceiling. Remember? Who'd have guessed The Old Man would rise up and turn into a boffin? With enough of the Filthy Stuff to spare? Pity he never did it when you were with us! His legs are weak, and he uses a stick, but he makes a few more steps everyday. He says it's painful. It happened when the house nearly caught fire. There was a piece in the Birmingham Mail about it. Val was on the floor, feeling the baby coming, and suddenly, there he was – on his bloody feet! We couldn't believe it! After all these years! But between you and me, I think he sees a lot of you in Val, and he thought (I know it sounds daft, but I don't know how else to put it) he thought it was you he was losing, all over again! He couldn't help it. He just stood up! Ever since that moment in the hallway, he seems to have accepted everything he fought against before, accepted that you aren't with us any more, like he never did up till now, as well as the baby daughter we lost, the sister I never saw. If that doesn't make sense, I can't help it; because that's how it looks to me. But you'll know what to make of it. You always do.*

'*I handed in my notice to The General nearly two months ago. One more to D-day! She wasn't at all upset about it. Nor was I. What I'm going to do for a job, God alone knows! Any suggestions? Nobody's got a vacancy that's shaped like Arnold Jonty, not even for board and lodging only; not that I could take it on now, with Val and The Bairn. Of course, I could go in with Dad; but I've got no head for figures. Not that kind, anyway. Let's hope something turns up.*

'*You'll be glad to hear that my urticaria pigmentosa is clearing up nicely and I've put on a bit of weight.*

'What would you do about Bennet's Folly? I love it. So does Dad. You know why: it's a gesture of defiance! The building, the fabric, everything. It genuflects – well, not a genuflexion, really. As they say in the army, it's mute insolence – more like! – before the officers of bastardy, and it cocks a snook at the false respectability and smugness established everywhere, and all the values we hate. In the front, it gives the usual salute; but behind its back, it is holding up two fingers, in a real Churchillian obscenity. (Like him, Mr Bennet loves panache.) But, inside, inside, it's itself! Irrepressible, vulgar, unregenerate, vigorous. You know! Although I'm not sure that Val likes it here that much. It makes work for her. Otherwise, she doesn't mind, but it goes against her training. And, anyway, there's The Bairn now: she alters a lot of things. Most. What would you do, Ma?

'I somehow feel you won't be hearing from me again. I guess you'll know why. But this one, Ma, I'd like you to get. The trouble is, I've got no address to send it where it can reach you. I'm hoping you've got ways and means of your own. That's what I've always hoped, anyway, with all the others, and they seemed to work all right. It's not that I don't love you any more. There will always be that. We both know about that, don't we? It's just – I think I've come at last where I know you would want me to be. And it's because of you and Val that it's happened. Of late, particularly. I couldn't have got here alone. Possessing her, and her possessing me, has somehow brought me to possess myself. Do you know what I mean? It's given me a something, a sweetness in my soul. Sorry about that! I shouldn't apologise to you about words like 'soul', I know. But, for me, it sounds so bloody highflown! Yet, it's the only word I know that will do. 'Mind' is no good! 'Psyche' is no good! 'Heart' is no good! 'Being' is no good! This is the only word I know for what I'm referring to. And I might as damn' well use it. Soul! There! I've done it.

'Ma, wherever you are, look after yourself! We'll think of you – often.

'Your loving son, daughter, granddaughter and Old Man.

Arnold.'

As Jonty completed the letter in his head, he felt that he wanted to write this one down. What he would do with it when he had, he didn't know. But the impulse was strong. So he decided to find a sheet or two and put it on paper while it was still fresh in his memory.

As he left his painting, and turned towards the high stone steps of Mr Bennet's cellar, he caught the faint sound of voices from the kitchen upstairs. He thought he detected excitement in them. And they weren't just the voices of Valerie and his father, either...

Had The Bairn turned into a ventriloquist?...

If not, they must have received visitors.

Who would want to visit them here, even if they knew about Bennet's Folly, which they didn't...

Had General Clatworthy discovered his address and determined to bring her Board of Governors to 5 Griffield Road, as well as a chosen band of colleagues, probably headed by the Reverend Heffler, to prove to them the unacceptable squalor that one of her housecraft staff had been living in?

Would she recommend a good brand of disinfectant?

She would certainly discover he was living with Valerie.

Would she know a remedy for the snails?

And she would find out about The Bairn.

Did she know anything about tropical fungi and untropical mushrooms? (As well as having to cope with Jonty Senior.)

Would she insist on Jonty himself giving a full report at the Staff Meeting next month? Or would she advise the Authorities to demolish Bennet's Folly completely?

'Now, stop it!' he told himself. 'There are only one or two extra voices. Or even one. It's a man's voice. Deep. Maybe it's old Bennet, asking for his cot back? Or, more like it, his rent!'

Jonty crept up the steps like a conspirator.

At the top, the cellar door opened into the passageway; he widened it carefully and tiptoed towards the kitchen, listening against the door.

For God's sake—! He could scarcely believe his ears.

Jonty flung it open.

"How on earth did you people get here?" he exclaimed, bursting into the kitchen. "Yasus! Am I glad to see a human being or two?"

"Human being yourself!" came the reply.

"You're fatter!" said Jonty.

"So are you!"

Jonty looked at Valerie in pleasure and triumph, and she looked back at him with an amused fondness.

He couldn't speak, he felt so full.

He grabbed the hand of Twaggin and pumped it up and down in silence, as if waiting for water to start spurting down his nostrils.

He went across to Soapy and kissed her on both cheeks. He smiled at his Dad. He didn't utter a sound. In his excitement, he had nearly smiled at Soapy and kissed the cheeks of Tom.

He turned to Valerie and put his arm round her shoulders, protectively, lovingly. She snuggled herself against him.

"This is Valerie," said Jonty, at last.

He didn't know what else to say.

"We know!" said Soapy. "Your father introduced us."

"I've been telling them about the fire," said Jonty Senior. "And the bit in the paper about the house nearly burning down."

"And about him walking again," said Soapy.

Just as neat as ever. Just as quiet. Just as positive. Just as devoted to the Archbishop and his short thighs. Yasus! It was good to see them.

"Well, sit down, and we'll have some beer!" said Jonty.

"Now, you're talking!" said Twaggin.

"I don't know where you're all going to sit. But we'll find somewhere," said Valerie.

"There's always the floor," said Soapy.

And she was as good as her word. She smoothed her skirt into a large hollow between her knees, sitting in the lotus position that Jonty remembered so well.

Twaggin tried to follow suit, but had the usual difficulty with the length of his thighs, and the tightness of his trousers. Eventually, lowering himself gingerly to the floor, he managed something like it, but he looked far from comfortable.

"Oh, well, if you're sure—," began Valerie.

"We're sure!" said Soapy.

"Lean against the wall. There!" said Jonty, indicating a space near to the stove that Twaggin would like. "It'll only fall down."

"I think I will," he said, thankfully. "We'll clean up later."

"I'll get the beer, then," said Jonty.

He returned from the scullery, putting the bottles on the long table. He opened them, and began to pour.

He felt wonderfully pleased to be doing it again for Soapy and Twaggin, and his pleasure was heightened by the presence of his father, Valerie and The Bairn. There was a delightful rightness about it, for him.

"Shall I pour one for her?" asked Jonty, out of his exuberance of spirit, nodding in the direction of The Bairn where she was sleeping peacefully in a clothesbasket.

"Don't you dare!" said Valerie.

"It's Tolley," he said

"Home from home!" said Twaggin.

"How'd you know where we lived?" he asked.

"Valerie wrote us a card from the hospital, telling us about the baby. We've been dying to met them both," answered Soapy.

"I didn't even know you knew where they lived, Val!" said Jonty.

"I wrote to your old college and they sent it on."

"You didn't tell me!"

"No! I didn't. I wanted it to be a surprise."

"Well, it certainly is!" said Jonty with a laugh. "Here's your beer!"

"Thanks!" said Soapy.

"My God!" said Twaggin, in disgust. "Coffee mugs! What's happened to?"

"—Behave yourself!" said Soapy, looking at Valerie.

Valerie smiled.

"Well, I'm buggered!" said Twaggin, in disapproval.

"Yes, you are!" said Soapy. "So get on with it!"

"Get on with what?" asked Twaggin, indignantly. "I'm drinking it as fast as I can!"

Soapy just regarded him with her wide steady gaze, inscrutable as a cat.

"Oh, yes! I see," said Twaggin, putting down his mug.

He wriggled his bottom, twitched his nose, and smoothed down his beard before starting to speak, just to show how important it was going to be.

"Well?" prodded Soapy.

"I've got a proposition to make to you two," he said, *basso profundo*. He looked across at Tom Jonty. "Three, if you like," he added.

"What about?" asked Jonty, suspiciously.

"It's all to do with the future," said Twaggin, mysteriously.

"As long as it isn't to do with the past," replied Jonty.

"That as well, partly."

"Oh, Yasus!" said Jonty.

"What's the proposition?" asked Valerie.

"Well," Twaggin began, "it's like this..."

As Twaggin talked, Jonty glanced at Soapy, who winked at him with a beautiful calmness.

He looked across at Valerie and smiled at her, happily; in her face a radiance answered to everything that was in him.

His feelings became as birds: they stretched their wings, gave a little leap onto the air, and flew.

About the Author

R oy Holland was born in Birmingham. He went to Africa in 1966 to teach in the universities of the Boleswa countries. In 1971 he went to Greece for three years. He and his family lived on the island of Levkas for six months, the Gulf of Corinth for a similar period, and in Corfu for a little over two years. He wrote full-time until 1974, when he returned to the U.K. and worked on a research project until returning to Africa in 1977. Thereafter he lived in Southern Africa and worked in universities in Zimbabwe, Lebowa and Venda. He was Professor of English at the University of the North, the University of Venda, as well as Dean of the Faculty of Arts in the later 80's. He retired early to write full-time, and now lives in Ledbury, Herefordshire.